TRIPTICKS

TRIPTICKS

Ann Quin

Introduced by Danielle Dutton

SHEFFIELD – LONDON – NEW YORK

And Other Stories
Sheffield – London – New York
www.andotherstories.org

First published in 1972 by Calder and Boyars Ltd
This edition published in 2022 by And Other Stories

9 8 7 6 5 4 3 2

ISBN: 9781913505400
eBook ISBN: 9781913505417

Cover Design: Ronaldo Alves after a Quin series design by Edward Bettison. Printed and bound by the CPI Group (UK) Ltd, Croydon, CR0 4YY.

A catalogue record for this book is available from the British Library.

And Other Stories gratefully acknowledge that our work is supported using public funding by Arts Council England.

Supported using public funding by
ARTS COUNCIL
ENGLAND

MIX
Paper from
responsible sources
FSC® C013604

INTRODUCTION

In 1968, the British literary quarterly *Ambit*, under the editorial auspices of J. G. Ballard, Edwin Brock, and Martin Bax, ran an infamous competition for the best work written under the influence of drugs. Years later, in an interview for the *Paris Review*, Ballard recalled that, overall, in terms of quality, "cannabis was the best stimulant, though some good pieces came out of LSD." But "the best writing of all," he went on, "was done by Ann Quin, under the influence of the contraceptive pill." This winning story, "Tripticks"—the beginning of the novel you're holding, which Quin had started earlier that year—won publication in the magazine and a prize for its author of £40. It's a funny little anecdote—"Don't laugh," Quin wrote to Marion Boyars, "but I've won a Drugs competition"—but it seems to me this comic subversion of *Ambit*'s contest is also a preview of the more serious subversive work Quin was doing in this book. For just as her birth-control pills—Orthonovin 2, to be specific—deflate the romantic narrative of 1960s drug culture, *Tripticks*, Quin's most pointedly satirical work, is a feminist anti-romance, anti-road novel of a distinctly disruptive sort.

Ann Quin was born in the English seaside town of Brighton in 1936 and died in 1973 having walked into the water. According to one newspaper report, her body was found floating off the coast of nearby Shoreham "dressed only in panties." A fisherman had seen her strip down on a Brighton beach the night before. The article is brief—"Sea-death woman was Brighton writer," it's called—but it includes a black-and-white photograph of Quin almost smiling beneath a dark pixie cut. "She wrote many books," the article concludes, "including *Berg* and *Three*." In fact, at the time of her death, Quin had published four extraordinary and stylistically daring novels: *Berg* (1964), *Three* (1966), *Passages* (1969), and *Tripticks* (1972). She was only thirty-seven years old.

You can read about her early years in "Leaving School—XI," an engaging autobiographical sketch included in 2018's *The Unmapped Country: Stories & Fragments,* edited by Jennifer Hodgson.* Quin's version of her own story begins after her working-class mother packed her off to a convent school to rid her of a Sussex accent and transform her into "a lady." In the convent she felt trapped, sensed the devil always near, "hiding in the folds of black cloth," and developed, "A death wish and a sense of sin. Also a great lust to find out, experience what evil really was." Naturally she escaped to a public library to read: Dostoyevsky, Elizabethan drama, Hardy, Lawrence, Woolf. "*The Waves,*" she says, "made me aware of the possibilities in writing." And how could it not? "The sun had not yet risen," Woolf begins. "The sea was indistinguishable from the sky, except that the sea was slightly creased as if a cloth had wrinkles in it. Gradually as the sky whitened a dark line lay on the horizon dividing the sea from the sky and the grey cloth became barred with thick strokes moving, one after another, beneath the surface, following each other, perusing each other perpetually."

Tripticks chronicles a nameless narrator's exploits as he drives across America pursuing his "No. 1 X-wife and her schoolboy gigolo"—or else the ex and her lover are pursuing him. Let's just say they're following each other, perpetually, in Buicks and Chevrolets, back and forth across a dystopian U.S.A. The America we find in Quin's novel is a place of rampant consumerism, religious hypocrisy, gory violence, and new-age self-help bullshit. It's also sex-mad, drug-addled, racist, and riddled with the language of advertising

*   Hodgson, who is currently writing a book about the life of Ann Quin, graciously answered several of my questions and shared some archival gems. I also want to gratefully acknowledge the archival work in Nonia Williams Korteling's "Designing its Own Shadow—Reading Ann Quin" and Dennis Cooper's blog spotlight page on *Tripticks*.

clichés. When we do glimpse the natural environment out a car or motel window, it is often almost terrifyingly beautiful, a not-quite-surreal prehistoric vastness of mesas and rock formations, "sheer walls of symmetrical blue grey basaltic columns" and "salt pools with crystals forming on their surfaces" and "bare broken peaks." But any romance of the American West is always immediately cut through, chopped down, pressed up against something else, like "6 packs of fridged beer" and a "U-Drive Inn" or a "lead-filled baseball bat" and a "hanging tree." Of course the setting of any novel, no matter how experimental, is made out of nothing but words, yet that truism feels somehow truer of *Tripticks*. Language is the landscape we're traversing in this book, a shifting vista of TV commercials, political rhetoric, sexual fantasy, and sand dunes. Language is what's *happening* in here.

The most stylistically daring of all of Quin's stylistically daring books, *Tripticks* also marks a departure. If Quin serves as a literary bridge between Virginia Woolf and Kathy Acker—as she's been described—then this is the book that gets her onto the Acker side of the canyon. Whereas her three previous novels showcase a quieter psychological interiority, here the prose is cacophonous and rude; it's fragmented by lists and quotations; it's polyvocal yet monologic, often funny, creatively punctuated, feels somehow both manic and static, and is, at times, so syntactically complex as to approach a ludic nonsense. In particular, much has been made of this book's linguistic relationship to the cut-up methods of William Burroughs. There's Ian Patterson in the *London Review of Books* noting that Quin used the techniques "of writers like Burroughs to create a fast-moving, jump-cutting, semi-absurd, road-trip quest narrative," and in the now defunct *Books and Bookmen* we're told *Tripticks* reads like "sub-Burrovian cut-uppery." *Publishers Weekly* argues more broadly that the book "evokes some of the more experimental Beat writers." Meanwhile, Becca Rothfeld in the *New York Review of Books* points out that Quin rejected any suspected Burrovian influence, but concludes: "*Tripticks* reads like a machismo mash-up by William Burroughs."

Personally, I read the book as a critique of machismo (Burrovian or otherwise). Machismo is self-romanticizing, after all, whereas everything about *Tripticks*, from those birth-control pills on down, reads like a subversion or parody of self-romance. We know via John Hall's 1972 "The Mighty Quin" that Quin did rely on "cut-ups from *Time*, *Life*, television commercials and Yankee sex and criminology pulp" while writing *Tripticks*, yet just as the novel is a parodic takedown of 1960s American culture that both mocks and engages seriously with the material of that culture, so too the book seems to me to simultaneously utilize the cut-up *and* to stand firmly outside the traditionally macho aesthetic with which it is associated. So while *Tripticks* can be read in relation to Burroughs, or, in a different way, to Kerouac's *On the Road* (another ostensibly drug-addled novel of the American "open road"), its relationship to these American cultural touchstones is not straightforward. It's worth noting that in 1961, in a letter to her friend Carol Burns, Quin wrote: "simply hating 'On the Road'—what a lot of sentimental rubbish and so tedious how it goes on and on in this phoney pseudo 'isn't life crazy but it's life man' sort of fashion." Also worth noting: as Quin was writing *Tripticks*, she was reading Gertrude Stein.

Then there are the images. Given the riotous linguistic performance of this book, it's tempting to want to read its illustrations for clues. Certainly I find myself reading in this way, looking back and forth between the images and text, hoping to find the one explicating the other. We're trained to expect illustrations to do exactly this. But while certain images here feel plainly illustrative, others seem only thematically related to the text's overall obsessions (maps, mesas, S&M), while still others come across as ambiguous or random (why so many gorillas?).

In an interview with Alan Burns, Carol Annand, the book's illustrator, explained that the text of *Tripticks* was already finished when she came on board to do the illustrations. In fact the book had already been accepted for publication, and so Annand had to fit her illustrations into an existing layout, hence images that frequently appear as footers, snuggled up against the pagination. This timing also likely explains why the book begins and ends with drawings, giving visual imagery both the first and final word. I'm especially interested in those closing panels: a hillside, a building, a rooftop. They don't match Quin's descriptions of the location of the novel's climactic closing scenes, even though there's also a rooftop involved in those shenanigans. Instead, Quin and Annand leave us with ambiguity, associative logic, more distance to cross. They leave us with collage, which, like so much in this book, relies for its effects on juxtaposition, a comedy of scale or tone, and an emphasis on messiness and chance. Annand, in that same interview, said she "tried to make a visual narrative run parallel with Ann's narrative." But Quin's is a narrative of disruption, quotation, and play; the images illustrate *that* as much as anything else.

In the end, *Tripticks* stands alone as Quin's only image-text collaboration—or at least the only one she published. Why did she decide on illustrations for this work? Was it to introduce another voice not her own, to expand the polyphony of the encounter? Or for the experience of collaboration? Or to build into *Tripticks* a greater sense of the materiality her text was already pursuing? For my part, I keep thinking back to that "drugs issue" of *Ambit*. If you look it up on their website you can flip through an old photographed copy priced at £40 (the same amount Quin won in the contest). Scroll through to the first page of "Tripticks" and you'll see it appears on a recto while facing it on the verso is a full page of inky black cartoonish drawings by an artist named Martin Leman. Perhaps Quin, having seen that spread, could never quite shake from "Tripticks"/*Tripticks* the playfully cacophonous energy of the image-text encounter.

In a piece at the *Quarterly Conversation*, Jesse Kohn, thinking through *Tripticks*'s stylistic difference from Quin's previous novels, writes: "As a writer with three books behind her, Quin seems as eager as the No 1. X-wife to blot out the memory of her previous cohort." By "previous cohort" he means, of course, *Berg*, *Three*, and *Passages*. Quin "flees stylistically" in *Tripticks*, Kohn argues, turning to face those previous three works just as our narrator "steer[s] his car towards the incensed trio of castrating X-wives." It's a neat idea—the fourth book bearing down on the earlier three like some sort of crazed mutineer—at least in part because it's natural to think of *Tripticks* as Quin's last stand, an end. In fact, Quin was working on a new novel when she died, and that work-in-progress, "The Unmapped Country," shows her operating more in the mode of her previous books than in any new artistic space *Tripticks* had opened up. Rather than representing an entirely new and final direction, then, it's possible to see *Tripticks* more like a wild U-turn, an outlier among outliers, Quin's own rebel work.

Danielle Dutton, St. Louis, 2022

TRIPTICKS

For Alan and Carol Burns

I have many names. Many faces. At the moment my No. 1 X-wife and her schoolboy gigolo are following a particularity of flesh attired in a grey suit and button-down Brooks Brothers shirt. Time checked 14.04 hours Central Standard Time. 73 degrees outside. Area 158,693 square miles, of which 1,890 square miles are water. Natural endowments are included in 20 million acres of public reservations.

All outdoor sports are possible. Deep sea sleeping,
and angling for small game are favourite pastimes.
The man who doesn't reckon his pleasures on a silver
platter is a fish that walks by night. Batman's the
name, reform's the game. Farm out the elite, the
Ruff-puffs, stinking thinking, temper tantrums, strong
winds, captivating experiences, Burn Down Peyton
Place, and inhale deeply stretched time with red eyes.

Eyes that fall away to 282 feet below sea level. I am
hunted by bear, mountain lion, elk and deer. Duck,
pheasant, rabbit, dove and quail. He at first feels a
little like George Custer at Little Big Horn. The enemy
is all around and awesome. The road ahead is going to
be difficult there will be some nervous Nellies and
some will become frustrated and bothered and break
ranks under the strain, and there will be blood, irony
dwarfs and dragons, skyrockets fired to celebrate
orgasm's efficiency. Suicide in a scented Sodom. Soul
on acid. Hero angelic, domestic and cosmic on a
journey with God on my side and the Brownie Troop.

Meanwhile I eat a toasted cheese hamburger, and dwell
on five days of unconfined feasts of roasted pig. A
miracle for a man who has nothing to lose. True your
family adventures may not match those of ancient
Greece, but you're equipped to make history and why
shouldn't you be, we've worked hard to make it that
way, we took no short cuts, spared no expense,
watched no clock. If you come filled with dreams it
may happen that your dream changes about every 15
minutes. The most is yet to come. 3,000 miles of
strawberry ice cream. Lips are frenchfries teasing
cole slaw fingers. My belly a Golden Poppy and the
Motto is I Have Yet To Find It. Or as posted to my
3 X-wives. Ranked according to value
vehicles
food
allied products

8

fabricated metal
machinery
stone
clay
glass
lumber and apparel.

White gold her hair one of my faces married (I displayed
at that time a droopy Stephen Crane moustache and
shiny eyes fixed on some wild interior vision). A bevy
of stars, many now fallen. Reproductions
a gristmill
wine press
and the reservoir with its undershot waterwheel, a
restored chapel and adjoining wing of seven rooms she
has taken over with the fourth husband of my No. 2
wife. Under the rough hewn redwood timbers they were
lashed together with rawhide. Open during daylight
hours an unusual arrangement of garden pools. Hours
subject to change in summer. No dogs, with the
exception of seeing-eye dogs, are allowed. Cats are
permitted to stay overnight provided they are on a
leash. A naturalist is on duty. As members of the 89-
person party died, those remaining resorted to
cannibalism. Only 47 were rescued. Picnicking. Campsites near the original area. Where I waited.
Cement
sand
gravel
and a gun.
Full of booze and passion for justice he sees himself
as a law and ardour candidate. His politics are
symbolized by the itchy trigger finger, and his judicial
philosophy is summed up in a tidy homily, 'You can't
serve papers on a rat'. For months he terrorized the
young women, and he was quickly dubbed the 'Phantom
Rapist'. He left typewritten notes at the scenes of his
crimes. A strategy he called 'working the system'.

He is layin' low, like Br'er Rabbit in his briar patch but we know he s in there. Hovering, pale and jittery, like an image that persists for a second after the set has been turned off.

I knew they scrutinized me through a two-way mirror. A matter of impatience between us. Between the sunken gardens, colonnade and the workshop. They set up their own quarantine regulations. Frozen turkeys and yoghourt delivered from the nearest Piggly Wiggly. She played the mechanical organ, he an old horse fiddle, and other games with other interesting relics. Most of their amusements, I soon realized, could be accommodated without my presence. The inertia of distant omniscient perspective. That other side of the goddamn appletree. Intimations of immortality and a need for sincerity and violence become reflections of the reality only. I know not what course others may take; but as for me, give me liberty or give me death. The attacker may be a sadist who bites slowly and intentionally, leaving well-defined teeth marks. Mainly found on the breast, neck, cheek, top of arm etc. Their degree of viciousness can vary tremendously, from the nipples being completely bitten off to one bite only, a 'love nip'.

I fired three times at their flagstone barbecue pit. And emerged from an underground channel through different rock strata. The name is not Gnome. The sensible thing is to kill them off, petrol bombs you know. Napalm your Castle awaits you.

It was when hitting Highway 101 I noticed they were following. I turned off into a winding road. Without
campsites
rest areas
picnicking
trailer hookups
Naturalist programme.

Their faces, glass faces behind me, twisted into grotesque shapes by the Pacific winds. Surrounded by Himalayan cedars, illuminated with 8,000 coloured lights. I proceeded with lights extinguished for several miles, and began a journey in an atomic submarine, scientifically authentic, to view mermaids, sea serpents, and the face of my first wife's father. Pets may be left in a kennel at the main gate, he said. This one happens to be dead, I replied. In that case we'll arrange a funeral at once. But I didn't want a burial performed just then. However I told him that eventually a statue in her honour would be appropriate for erection in the town park, where visitors may choose to arrive by helicopters. He seemed genuinely pleased at this idea and showed me around the grounds of his No. 1 home. In addition to the eight-room stone and frame house (a market value of $82,000 when it was appraised six years ago he confidentially told me) there were a grassy helicopter pad, a log-cabin guest house, two boathouses, a kidney-shaped swimming pool, a sauna, a trampoline and a profusion of trees and marigolds. 'All this was pasture, plain pasture when we bought it, I planted those pines as little sprouts and look at them now, you have to keep them fertilized and use lots of mulch.' A recent hailstorm had played havoc with the trees and the roof of the house. He noted aloud 'I've got to fix that'. He bent over and picked up several broken willow branches and handed them to his chauffeur (who I felt sure secretly belonged to the Panthers). While an electric player piano blared Oklahoma he led me to the garage where there were three autos:
a 1926 model T Ford
1930 Model A
A new red convertible. 'A copy,' he said proudly, 'of the '29 Ford Phieton.' He tried to start the Model T, but the motor coughed, spat and died. 'Someone's been tinkering at the choke.' He hopped out, lifted the

hood and tinkered for a minute, explaining that he used to run a bike repair shop and liked doing his own mechanical work. Then his ire was directed at his anti-smog gadget. 'The car idles so fast that it automatically leaps to 30 miles an hour when I take my foot off the brake, I've got to be careful I don't kill somebody,' he said with a rueful smile 'just coming out of my drive.'

He led me further into the grounds. Crocodiles, hippopotami, and snakes slipped through murky water. Along the shore, amid live, rare tropical trees, shrubs, and flowers, appeared elephants and other jungle animals. 'Visitors you know will find it hard to believe that none of the animals are alive.' I felt convinced one or two were, possibly his wife's pets. She took her poodle Bu-Bu with her everywhere. 'I wish I had been an Edwardian,' she moaned at dinner on my first visit. 'When we give a dinner party as you can see the people who serve wear green jackets and white gloves, but look at the curtains they're in shreds. 'That naughty Bu-Bu of yours,' her husband shouted.

After dinner he showed me the champagne plant, wine cellars and bottling rooms. This was just a hobby, he explained. He was in the ballpen industry, with eighteen plants selling a billion ballpoints a year in 96 countries, 'enough to pen a letter stretching from here to Saturn'. I knew the familiar commercials: a ballpoint being buried by a bulldozer, rattled on a flamenco dancer's boot and shot from a rifle, only to write perfectly again. He claimed that it would soon make the pencil obsolete.

I saw myself in the near future living like a modern pasha. Indulging an insatiable yen for the luxuries a Falcon jet
Convair turbo-prop
Jet Commander

Rolls-Royce
Custom Lincoln
Caddy
Sting Ray
a houseboat
and a Riva speedboat, and perhaps a thoroughbred
racing stable, and two Eliza Doolittles for maids.

A recent afternoon in his life. Man Friday helps him
into his Pierre Cardin jacket. The Rolls is waiting.
Three lissom girls are already in the back seat. He
wanders across the lawn to pet his two tame ocelots.
'Tell my wife that I'll be back tomorrow.' The Rolls
is crunching along the gravel driveway when someone
runs from the house and shouts, 'Urgent call from
New York.' Twenty minutes later he is finally airborne
in his twin engine falcon jet.

I tentatively asked him about his earnings. 'Now you're
prying into my personal business,' was his angry retort.
'Just say it's between 50 cents and 5 million dollars.'
Then he went on about a fund he was creating to provide
huge public cocktail parties with free food and drink
for anyone who wants to attend. 'This would be a real
nice way to be remembered,' he said. There had to be
a hitch - the parties would not start till after his
death, and he wants to enjoy them too. So, for every
party, he has arranged with a local funeral home to
have his remains wheeled out in a big silver casket.
'They will stay at the party until the last guest has
gone.' As he told me all this he had the strangest
gleam in his eyes, it was like he couldn't wait to die
and get on with the fun.

His study was built in the shape of a wine barrel. He
showed me photographs of his daughter in graduation
drag. Of her as a plump baby, naked on a crocodile
skin. And photos of his home town
pharmacy

14

ice cream parlour
bank
drugstore
dentist's office
general store
an old oil rig
early locomotive
box-car
handcar and caboose
hotel
saloon and other enterprises.

I became the caricature of the surly inarticulate 'man,
like I mean', as I caught sight of his daughter, my
first wife to be, chewing gum in the memorial garden
of camelias, roses and flowering shrubs. A maze
symbolizing the various paths offered in life. At its
centre a small stone summerhouse with a highly
finished interior signifying the hastiness of judgment
on the basis of outward appearances.

'That's the orchard over there a fine sight to see you
know,' he said, 'the Cherry Picking Festival is held
in June and the public is invited to pick their own fruit,
and over there well we have the Marine Corps Supply
Depot - there we go you know my grandmother or was
it my great grandfather was Celtic see that fireplace
well its modelled after a Scottish war lord's and this
well it's a miniature Railway an authentic replica you
know of an oldtime coal-burning engine and that well
that's a photo of the world's largest jet-missile rocket
test centre and has a 22-mile runway - not open to
visitors of course.'

I made the appropriate gestures, remarks, while
thinking of his daughter's petrified face imprinted on
fossilized leaves. Vital secrets of her own wondering
aloud while shopping by Rolls. I was curious to know
if she was a member, like her mother, of the D.R.

(Daughters of the Revolution). I doubted it. Her speciality would be wooden heads, tightly leather-wrapped. At the moment, her father reported, she was preoccupied with lizards, which she says 'look like man in certain stages'.

Later at a health resort under hot-water geysers we made it for the first time in the mineral springs and mineralized mud baths. My mouth searching for hers by means of siphon pipes. And later that same day I got a strange blow-job in a parking lot, it was 35 degrees outside, by a weird woman, two days later I was still weak at the knees and couldn't think about it. Now I could try and ease my way out of this by saying I didn't ask questions, just stated my personality

smart, well-educated	Lack of respect for authority
ambitious	lack of spiritual and moral
deep concern for social	fibre
problems	lack of responsibility
good values, character	lack of manners
communicate	lack of dialogue with elders
independent thinker	values ill-defined
poised personality	lack of good study habits
vocal, will speak up	lack of love for fellow men
mature, prepared for	lack of self-respect
life	too impetuous
versatile, able	too introspective
intellectually curious	too introspective
well-groomed	nothing missing
care about community	

read for pleasure
consider myself informed
sense of humour is important
enjoy discussing ideas
my best work is done when I'm not working
I am dominant
relationship with my family is fucked up

I am sophisticated
considered attractive
interested in marriage
liberal regarding sex
more of a dove than a hawk
my date should be psychologically weaker
I am optimistic
Pot and pop-pills are morally right
I drink regularly

On the other hand I am interested in some of the
factors which may, or may not, effect my psychological
feelings. For this reason I have hand exercise springs
REMEMBER
Hold the hand spring in a closed position throughout the
'thinking' period. Place your check mark on the line,
not in between lines

THIS	NOT THIS
X	X

Do Not Omit any Scales for Any Concept
Yesterday

Good				Bad
large				large
unpleasant				pleasant
light				heavy
cold				hot
active				passive
rough				smooth

My Mood Now

small	large
passive	active
hot	cold
bad	good
heavy	light
pleasant	unpleasant

Fantasy Profile

Organized	Dreamer	Athletic	Sexy
Confident	Aggressive	Subtle	Natural
Practical	Well-dressed	Healthy	Introverted
Passionate	Thrifty	Quiet	Nervous
Funny	Warm	Paternal	Extroverted
Serious	Impulsive	Talkative	Trusting
Active	Intelligent	Kind	Content
Maternal	Cheerful	Creative	Self-controlled
Cautious	Do-it-yourself	Altruistic	Emotional
Reflective	Jealous	Obsessive	Wholesome

Common Interests

Pets	Jazz	Psychology
Parties	Walking	Photography
Lectures	Scientific	E.S.P.
Medicine	journals	Stock Market
Stereo	Movies	Antiques
equipment	Yoga	Astrology
Acting	Humanities	Foreign travel
Modern lit.	Dancing	Sugar buns
Discotheques	Portable lawns	
Ethics		
Pop Art		

and unusual work-it-yourself devices

Still what have I managed to say - that this is a
performance of extraordinary charm and brilliant
technique. And though there are dozens of qualities I
value more, this production embodies its own vision
as completely as any I have ever seen. Certainly my
No. 1 wife had some of these qualities, concepts, and
I recognize now only too well that large, active,
flushed face following me round every bend. Along the
northeastern edge of the city. Round the remains of
a 11-feet in diameter valley oak, killed by miners
digging around its roots for gold. She failed seeing
me then as they both marvelled at the two pieces of

tree preserved in the monument. But as soon as I climbed into the Chevy they began the chase again.

He rages across the country like a sorcerer's apprentice with a gunmetal wand. This puffy-eyed, ponch-jowled hero has vague stirrings of honour and mortality. He knows he is superannuated just as Randolph Scott did in Ride the High Country, but he rides the low country with nowhere to go but lower.

A broad expanse of white sand beach, bordered by Monterey cypress trees. I left the Chevy in a prominent place outside the U-Drive Inn. On returning I noticed they had changed their name for the register. I recognised his cramped writing. Through the keyhole I watched them doing Yoga together. They were naked. Why had she never done that with me? Admittedly there had been some extraordinary positions we discovered. Obviously anything in three dimensions can be any shape, regular or irregular, and can have any relation to the wall, floor, ceiling, room, rooms or exterior or none at all. No proscenium arch is able to limit the variables of action. An infinite variety of angles and perspectives. Cannot be identified, does not affirm any order but has its own interelation of parts, colour, scale and touch.

Eerie rites greet the morning sun. He kneels on the floor grasping a small wheel with both hands and slowly prostrates himself. On a roof not far away someone runs on a treadmill. The president of a dressmaking company puts on a belt that sends electric shocks into his abdomen, while his wife stands with one foot on a four-wheeled board and the other foot on another four-wheeled board reverently squatting and rising, while their daughter lies head down on a slanted board, jerking convulsively at the waist. Sauna belts to sweat into. Executive Barbells to swing. Tensolators for building up muscles;

vibrator massage machines ('both centrifugal and percussion action') and roller massage machines ('for deep-penetrating massage') treadmills and rocks and vibrating belts and electric bicycles ('Do your story dictation aboard a Trimcycle'). Tone-O-Matic weighted belts - belts loaded with 10 pounds of lead and intended to be worn in the normal course of a day's activity. One man cried that his hands were getting bigger and bigger. Instructional manuals in such arts as giving a massage ('People rubbing people is always nice. People rubbing people with skill is an order of magnitude nicer').

Through another keyhole I had watched my No. 2 wife being whipped with kippers, imported from Scotland. I thought then goddamit why hadn't she ever told me? The kippers were never mentioned in the divorce proceedings, her Attorney was an understanding guy, or so she informed me in the middle of one of our last fights. Oh those beautiful silent battles on the bed when finally I would get her across my knees - ah well... Yes her Attorney, the one who used the kippers, she also informed me he liked fishing for black bass
bluegill
crappie
and catfish
And came from a once booming mining town, complete with plaza and hanging tree. His father kept a saloon sporting batwing doors, housing firearms, coins, minerals and other documents, papers of historical interest. I always knew she had an interest in antiques. He was well-preserved, I guess, for his age. Maybe the dieting and the wearing of a Tone-O-Matic weighted belt helped.

Meanwhile my No. 1 wife and her lover kept me awake half the night. Why hadn't she ever moaned like that with me? What I needed, of course, was a Spy-Prober,

one that penetrates solid barriers, makes any wall
an open door. Yes, it even looks DOWN into a room
below. A 3 precision ground optical quality lenses,
affording an extreme wide angle field on objects
standing by the very wall through which you are
observing. Such sharp delineation that you can
photograph right through it, sharply recording everything in the viewed area. Looks like an ordinary pen
when carried in your pocket (had my father-in-law
thought of that one?) And for those of you who demand
perfection, a professional model complete with silent
hidden drill. As countless people have shown, the
individual need not really be powerless, the machine
can be made to stop and change direction, even though
Talking Turk knows your secrets.

All right now so why are you confused? You have barely
lived yet life, you feel, has already passed you by.
Another inevitable victim, the non-spy who has never
paid any attention to cryptography, a pragmatist who
doesn't know on which side his corn bread is buttered.
What began as a quiet investigation has blown into a
full-scale and still unresolved controversy. Sample
question: How do you respond to those who present
you as a conk-headed junkie, fanatical and depopulating
the Centre? With these characteristics in mind
researchers have been working on a variety of complex
experiments designed to detect desperate and
imaginative efforts in stuffy motels filled with
nightmares and gentle but impassioned ladies, and
other critical areas. They have used giant fans, rotating
racks, poem-snippets in fog machines, sugar buns
dropped from planes, or spewed upward from strange
machines. One of these an E-meter can not only detect
unhealthy habit patterns during the oedipal period, but
can also pick up subtle emanations from a tomato.
The E-meters and their accompanying leaflets are
protected from seizure by the right of freedom of

worship, which puts them beyond the reach of The
Man from U.N.C.L.E. and the F.D.A. They are not
used to diagnose or treat physical disease, or Lunar
Microbe hunters, they are treating the spirit of
laconic lovers with falsetto voices. They are qualified
to perform shirt open gospel rock, barnyard baths,
familiarization flights and burial rites. But think about
what's really wrong with today's calculators, think
about a calculator which eliminates all the things you
don't like:
The immaculate silhouettes
60 relatives
Snoopy's mother
Britain's Bonnie Prince
The New lunatics
Four wives at a time
Improbable satyrs
Unhip hippies
Little Carlo
And egg communication

I mapped out the next day's route, making sure to
supply myself with extra water. The thought of the
three of us splitting into frantic parties, each striving
wildly to get out of the barren valley finally made me
have a peaceful sleep. I dreamed of being a love slave
to a gang of outlaw women. Ah those cabinets of
dreams. Always the hero to the rescue of wonder
women who were continually being molested by
giant lizards
snared by dissolute white slavers aboard a baroque
submarine
enslaved in an Albanian bauxite mine
sacrificed by a sacred polar bear
cultivated by a mad fungologist
hostess to a tupperware party in Kew Gardens
slain by a blind zen archer
attacked by a pack of half-starved gila monsters

22

given a 3-year gift subscription to 'Family Circle'
magazine
mailed to Ceylon
belaboured by a deranged ex-Nazi
tied to a Japanese monorail
abducted by a secret society of midwestern necro-
philiacs
dangled from a rope above steaming tarpits
fired at by a manta ray
elected recording secretary of the Local Weight
Watcher's Club
crucified by a degenerate rabbi
made cruel sport of by a band of incredible lesbians
captured by a warped Macao tattoo artist
set upon by an enormous scorpion
subjected to the aberrant whims of a crazed Brazilian
foot fetishist
resurrected by a maniacal Eskimo medicine man
tuned in every afternoon at four o'clock to watch The
Dating Game
assaulted by Zeppelins
abducted by U.F.O.
High Priestess to the black Falashas of Ethiopia.

What man can resist the siren song of sex? Down
through the ages, feminine wiles have brought mighty
men to their knees, empires have been lost and
reputations have been ruined by temptresses who have
seduced the gullible to gain what they desire, and then
consign their hapless victims to a destiny of doom!
Only recently a blonde beauty whispered sweet
promises to a lonely bachelor and lured him to a
desolate spot where, instead of fulfilling his desires,
she delivered him into the arms of death. At one
point when the victim-to-be showed signs of losing
interest in the blandishments of the sirens, the girls
put on an impromptu performance that made Salome's
dance of the seven veils resemble a Girl Scout's

23

festival.

The Weather Bureau reported it had been as high as 120 degrees for days in succession. At sunrise I turned off the highway and started crossing the valley. I saw they were hesitant, he hunched over the wheel, while she sat on a bench in the picnicking area, scraping off her already dry pancake makeup. Those hollow spheres with centres of quartzlike material formed by particles of lime. Soon I couldn't see them at all for the rising dust. Then dream shapes formed out of the desert, and their Buick floated a few miles behind me. I didn't have the energy or patience to view the wealth of geological phenomena, but was well aware of the divisions of time, the space that widened, narrowed between the present and the past. Memories held together by the thinnest of threads, nevertheless self-contained and delicious, sunny, boisterous and ironic. They melted, melded and interfused with 1,000 plastic egg-shapes suspended into beautiful buoyancies of chinchilla clouds. Instead of a battlefield, the arena became a dance floor, which did not in any way alleviate or moderate the risks involved. Memories that used to communicate a violent anxiety in the valley created an airy sense of freedom, light and light-heartedness. Texture, trigger, tonality all pink, soft and glowing. Why not see for yourself a different big scene (for a nominal extra charge) that whirls you as if you were on a carousel, or you'll be submerged to watch the sinking of an entire fleet, or taken atop a hill to see a fiery chariot in the clouds, robbers and upgrades, psychiatric drunks, pigs' voices and yearnings of youth.

Investigation but little action in cloud cuckooland, and it's the loneliest feeling in the world, you don't see anyone, the banks don't know you and who's going to give credit to a long-haired stranger from across the border? And why were there plasticine porters with

looking-glass ties as Murf the Surf came out carrying in his head a lurid crime. He planned the caper with movie rights in mind.

I decided it would be a stunning scientific and intellectual accomplishment for a creature who, in the space of a few million years - the bat of an eyelash in evolutionary accounting - emerged from the desert to hurl himself at two bodies. Its effects on human civilization would be a matter of conjecture. But it would in any event be a shining reaffirmation of the optimistic premise that whatever man imagines he can bring to pass.

I saw the headlines:
                    Dance, Strangler, Dance

He seemed to be a loveable clown, but she knew better.

He riddled their car with bullets, drove off with his screaming love captive.

The double murder had all the earmarks of a typical lover's lane sex crime. Yet there were certain angles that caused the police to wonder whether there was more to the case than met the eye...

It's difficult to imagine serene scene could be setting for tragedy. Corpse was found in creek behind bench.

They stage a modern Wild West drama that has everything - 110 m.p.h. running gunfights, full-speed crashes, through roadblocks, horseback posses with blood-hounds, a pretty blonde who knows plenty - and violent death in a mountain cave.

However at one point outside a ghost town I thought yes I could die here quite happily, no longer confuse the mainspring of the movement with the movement. And when he bleeds, falls and dies, he does so in a beautifully obscene slow motion, a star swimmer in his own aquacade of blood. A moment in death when the body no longer functions, when it becomes an

25

object and has a certain kind of detached ugly beauty.
And a tortured Earth Goddess with the shimmer of
luxurious shoulder-length gloves of stretch nylon
would lean over me, unbuttoning, folding back one of
her gloves to close my eyes. Smooth, resolved and
beautiful. The feel of history, the gloom chasers that
moved many a good man who fought fire and flood,
varmints and vermin, as region after region filled
with the settlers and homesteaders who proclaimed
We are breaking sod for unnumbered millions to come.
In the meantime there are places to go, things to
see, and the Daughters of Texas to meet. Everyone
should have the right to go to Heaven or Hell in his
own way. This simple remedy carried me through for
an hour or so. Now I enjoy violence as much as the
next guy, but enough is enough. Five days is plenty
for the most exciting series, and with the heat
penetrating my brain wires, and swelling my rocks, I
decided to turn back.

I passed them at 110 m.p.h. So I didn't have the chance
of seeing their white sun sunken faces turn crimson.
This is the sin of sins against an awkward power
structure. The refusal really to take the situation
seriously. However I still had the gun, though
unloaded, in case of any unforeseen advantage on their
side. Perhaps they had some odourless colourless
chemical flood that would make my pupils, bladder
and alimentary canal constrict, my penis erect, the
tear and saliva glands secrete, and my heart slow down.
I began feeling dizzy - perhaps the hamburger I had
eaten... I remembered at his last press conference
the President had recited an ode to the hot dog 'I come
from humble origins. Why, we were raised on hot
dogs and hamburgers. We've got to look after the hot dog.

The quantities now on hand were said to be modest, but
the Army has ample resources for fast mass production
whenever the need arises. Stored in sod-covered,

concrete 'igloos' they are kept in constant cycles of development, production, storage, elimination and replacement. Several of the installations have almost pastoral settings where game abounds and Boy Scouts come to camp and hike. Hamburgers and hot dogs are developed in laboratories with long stainless steel and sealed glass cabinets, many bearing stencilled nicknames like 'African Queenburger' and 'Tribulation Row'. Fertilized meat enters the labs in compartmented trays and moves through the cabinets on conveyor belts. As they pass the meat is infected by lab technicians working through the cabinet walls with heavy rubber gloves and hypodermic needles. Some of the processed material is used for test purposes. The remainder is frozen into pellets and hermetically sealed in containers for shipment to China. Prison inmates, and conscientious objectors are used to test the efficiency of the plant's products.

I felt as dry as a glassful of sand. They were still pursuing. They really were taking the whole thing very seriously. That worried me. The fact I could foresee them as a lost patrol chasing their chartered shadows through endless deserts. But then I would wave a flag, arrange for a brass band to play 'When Johnnie Comes Marching Home', and bring extra noisemakers, confetti, drink beer, kiss girls. There'd be songs, dancing, music, flowers, Japanese girls, werewolves in the organ, computerized companions and electronic breaks, a stretched version of retiring rooms with organic hair tonic, sleeps 15, or maybe 16 if there are two in the elliptical bed. A room with a built-in deluge, 7 layers of falsies, a rubber rear, the services of part-time married priests, a zoot-suited hustler and steaming Courtesans bending over hundreds of celebrities like Ho Chi Minh, Betty Grable, Lyndon Johnson, Regis Toomey, and John Wayne rising out of their ghost towns. Poking around he stumbled

upon an exquisitely poised unitary-body, an elusive
long-haired beauty trying to read Ho in the step-down
Roman bath. To capture the delicate self-sustaining
chain reactions he placed an attack trained Doberman
pinscher in her lap. A spiritual balance regained.

Those very words she used once as we lay sunning
ourselves by her daddy's kidney-shaped pool. I didn't
believe in her soul-saving outfit, at least not until
she undid her leather bikini. 'No I don't want to save
your soul I want to save your arse.' She was on one of
her amphetamine trips then, and possibly taking some
now before sucking him off to keep his driving spirits
up. Good God the thought of her doing that to anyone
but myself - there was nothing for it but he must go.
I just hoped he wasn't wearing a bullet-proof vest. But
he sat impassively watching his decision sinking surely
into oblivion. Like the apple of Sodom ('When grasped
by the hand it crumbled and dissolved into smoke and
ashes'.) Clearly fresh thinking was needed. People
are a bit like cars. They can't go on forever. Somewhere along the line, they're going to need a check-up,
a few repairs, and a rest, especially if an ominous
rattle seems to be developing.

I stood at the mouth of a creek and vomited over the
sign VISITORS SHOULD DRINK ONLY FROM CLEARLY
MARKED SPRINGS. At the visitor centre I noticed
daytime hourly
slide shows features
mountains
canyons
former centres of mining activities
crystal-like formations
salt pools with crystals forming on their surfaces
sand dunes
beehive charcoal kilns
deteriorated mining towns.

I felt sure somewhere inside would be her father posing as the Grandiose Inquisitor applying privileged powers dispensing ballpoint pens and lollipops. I slid through the air-conditioned dark into a brightly-lit room. On a platform sat a white-haired colonel. She had wall-to-wall hips, an ear-to-ear mouth, and more teeth than a pretzel has salt. 'How nice to see you here first time isn't it? Be sure to come back next year.' She launched into an impassioned plea, as I hovered in the doorway. 'Don't consider this just a pleasant day none of you is lost you only have to give yourself to Jesus isn't there one among you who wants to leave this life stand up and come to us.' I took a few steps further into the room. A spotlight fell instantly onto my face. 'I'm Murf the Surf and I'm the one they suspect of taking off the Star of India.' I said with a voice that oscillated from roar to squeak. Her engaging smile assured me that everything was arranged just for my comfort and pleasure. 'Why you're the kind of man who takes traveller's cheques to Santa Barbara,' she said with a quaint original voice that swung between ages 4 and 40. 'Where are our dreams,' she cried, 'we have lost our dreams and a country without dreams is already dead, but we can hold this sonuvabitch we can hold it till hell freezes solid against those who have opened the floodgates of pornography and unleashed a reign of terror upon law-abiding citizens.' I was handed a paperbound book with an uplifting thought for each day, a copy of the Strijdkreet (battlecry) of the Salvation Army's bimonthly and a handmade Christmas-decorated cardboard pyramid which turned out to hold candy. Later when I opened the book I found it was Mein Kampf and Der Führer hat immer Recht.

I emerged into the blinding yellow. They must have passed by, possibly back on the main road, having an argument. I thought I heard her hysterical voice, but it was a horse neighing. Her voice. Her mother's above the wedding march.

The bride wore a traditional long-sleeved full-length white satin wedding dress, and her seven bridesmaids were in pink silk trimmed with goya red velvet ribbons (subdued lest they clashed with the bridegroom's resplendent full dress uniform). The make-up man had gently vacuum pumped the bride's blackheads out, shaved her eyebrows, waxed her hairline to change the shape of her face. Raised and arched her eyebrows to open her eyes, and used $2\frac{1}{2}$ sets of eyelashes. Shaded her nose to make it look smaller and soften the lines around her mouth and cheeks. There was a six foot wedding cake and $5,000 dollars worth of champagne had been ordered. So the newspapers accounted for their wedding. The mother's face a wreath of smiles, at last my daughter has decided to keep the good life rolling in high gear.

Our elopement had never been condescended to. Without emerging from our $11 a day cave on the fourteenth (I knew it was really the thirteenth) of some hotel, we bribed them by call and collect. 'Oh leave it to me honey daddy will come round.' Fugitive lovers. She enjoyed it more. The 'phone calls, cables, letters. Demands. Commands. After a week the chauffeured limousine arrived with a note All is Forgiven Come Home. She went. I remained a further week until the limousine approached again. She sat between her parents looking like she'd come to pick up a corpse. 'I'm pregnant,' she said, as I climbed in next to their chauffeur.

We were legally joined at the nearest marriage mill that also catered for cremations. No 5-tiered pound cake topped with spun-sugar basket. No calligraphers, their labours done, studied their handiwork on 500 invitations and 'carriage cards' (for parking assignments). No aides clocked the ceremony in advance. Her father handed me the ring. Her mother a Wedding plaque Lovely Keepsake for Bride & Groom. Large 8" natural cork mat makes perfect anniv. gift too. Use as hot pad or wall decoration. Cute. And an aunt, who had been told, sent Baby's First shoes, Bronze-plated in solid metal.

The ceremony over in a few minutes. The divorce a year later took a little longer. About a day. I wasn't present. Her father's letter ended with No man need be our enemy, no one's interests need be forgotten. Because ours is the strength, ours also must be the generosity. I didn't cash the cheque but used it for other purposes. Independence of expression has now become almost unthinkable. Determine what forces are required and procure and support them as economically as possible.

The whole episode fragmented into a honeycomb of separate actions. Mock histrionics where her father prostrated himself before me, dug his nose in the rug, and moaned 'look please do what I say give my daughter up and you'll have an income of...' Plot diminishes in a forest of effects and accidents. Motivations done away with, loose ends ignored, as the son-in-law is invited to become the father's collaborator filling in the gaps he left out.

We lived in the annexe, or tried to. I took up:
Photography
Get away from the 'picture postcard' complex in your picture-making. Add human interest by placing members of the family in scenes of static subjects like buildings and monuments - above all have them doing something.

Hypnotism
Hypnotise self and others with the help of this

fascinating record. Side 1 puts others in a trance, passes control to you. Flip side for self-hypnosis, ends by giving suggestion to re-hypnotize yourself at will then awakens you. Fascinating echo-chamber background and free eye-fixation discs. Satisfaction guaranteed.

Pets

3 Pet seahorses and Free hitching post. Selected fresh caught live sent by air mail. A kit of Free food, hitching post and simple instructions for raising these exotic little pets in jar or fish bowl. The father gives birth to the young alive. Guaranteed live delivery.

Calisthenics

Start every day with a few minutes quick calisthenics. A dozen push-ups will loosen the muscles of your back and arms and thighs; the same number of sit-ups will, if practised religiously, place bands of iron across your middle. Round the calisthenic session off with a dozen toe-touches, making sure not to bend your knees.

Inventions

A voice recognition device, built into a computer to keep out intruders. Anybody requesting confidential information would have to talk into a microphone, connected to the computer. An unauthorized voice, not recognized by the device, would stand little chance of gaining access to the information.

Movie Making

She came on as the Statue of Liberty, crown and all, wrapped in some silver stuff. She stripped to some mind-breaking music, while film clips of people like the Pope and the President were projected behind her. For a climax she took a fall, breaking

the balloons which filled her bra and released red
paint, which she smeared over her body.

Fishing

The formal gardens contain a large amount of
interesting rockwork, as well as numerous varieties
of flowers. The fish in the enclosed area on the
lakeshore may be fed by hand.

The First Lady of my marital life wanting a fight for
equal rites other than keeping the country aware of Dike
protection seriously considered working for some large
goal such as the alleviation of hunger and setting up
food memorials. Her mother taking up her official
functions began decorating the baby's room in dervish
loops and attending fashion shows to benefit the
S.I.P.S.D.C. (Skills Improvement Programme for
State Department Clerks).

Meanwhile my father-in-law became totally dedicated
to the pursuit of a large, ill-tempered fighting fish
called the muskellunge, or muskie. The muskie
mystique makes frustration relatively easy to bear;
muskie charters generally pull away at the crack of
10 a.m. and return in time for cocktails. Two poles
are rigged to the back of the boat and he sits down to
drink, play cards or read. The boat rumbles along
at about 5 m.p.h., its artificial lures glittering in
the foam just behind the propellers, and quiet
descends - until the strike. He had a healthy respect
for the fish's ugly mouth lined with razor-sharp teeth.
He never pulls one in until he stashes its head with
a lead-filled baseball bat. His wife didn't like
fishing but one day decided to go aboard with him and
asked me to join them. Of course Bu-Bu came too.
Lady and poodle sulked in the cabin. Finally 'Daddy'
got a good-sized muskie on the line but the poodle
started biting him - so he grabbed Bu-Bu and threw
him overboard. His wife screamed 'save the dog' and

he yelled 'land the fish'. I figured it was his money, so we landed the fish. Later I swung the boat back, swooped up the dog in his net and dumped it damp and docile on deck. She started screaming out I had tried to kill her dog. He shouted that it was the first time in 5 years the dog wasn't barking and threatened to throw her in and silence her too, and muttered to me as he lovingly stroked the muskie's body, 'what my wife really needs is open-hearted surgery and they should go in through her feet'.

As summer passed the quartet became a tiny tribe, with increasing hysterical rituals of confession and conformity. Always, violence just a dare away. I can still hear his voice, and one of the first sermons he gave me in his oval room. 'The structure of our family has rested from the beginning on a foundation of moral purpose - the right to participate in decisions carries with it the duty to abide by those decisions when reached, recognizing that no one can have his own way all the time. ' What he failed to emphasize was that the realities of domestic power sometimes dilutes these principles. He did not really confront the challenge I had shown specifically where the system failed.

I ate, slept and worked in a suite on the east side of the house overlooking the swimming pool. Air-conditioning kept the temperature at a constant 70 degrees. A colour television set in the living-room, another in the bedroom, and two spares in case of breakdown. My diet consisted mostly of plain foods: well-done sirloin steaks, fruit and exactly seven figs for breakfast. While my wife and her mother knitted blue and pink baby gear and watched one or all the televisions. All night movies. Sleeping, complaining of feeling sick, headachey during the day.

I emerged from $2\frac{1}{2}$ months of 'married life' and

delivered an impressive speech in which I rejected the
idea of retiring in such a way at my age because
'there's no safety in hiding' and vowed to carry forward
special commitments to justice, excellence, and
courage. Hal the computer tries to take over, perhaps
it is really Moby Dick. There is a link here, he wants
to shake up TV and reform everything in sight. Even
the best fibre needs a world force behind it. We hate
to seem ostentatious, we have what I would call a
sequential polygamy happiness for small housewives.
No drippy laundry, polish once every 4 months and
lead the double life. Don't worry unless your stomach
turns purple, a new insecticide quickly and completely
eradicates household pests with patience pewter and
a thin coat of asphalt. They achieve a humble kind of
immortality. You press the button we do the rest, we
save you thinking with mind and heart. Remember
you're one of the family so be King for an hour or so.
Complain if the cushions are too soft, initial a few
state papers, call for champagne, chat with a
neighbouring princess, or stretch and sleep, you're
in a world made perfect for Kings screened from the
others. White smoke proves snorkels are working
well. Reconnaissance system spies out the secrets
of a beachfront and catches the brightest and faintest
stages of a nuclear blast. A cavernous vessel, a
ruddy satellite, the beginning of a life. Special
continuous loop tape switches tracks automatically for
uninterrupted listening pleasure as you operate simple
push-button on-and-off controls with one hand
exclusive. But don't forget to practise Enthusiasm
daily APRPBWPRAA (Affirmative Prayers Release
Powers By Which Positive Results Are Accomplished).
Take all your bills lay them out on the bed and then
ask God what to do about them ask Him for a definite
plan for eliminating comfortable fat matrons in
opulent costumes feelin' smellin' knowin' the corridors
of the heart. And if you think you'll have doubts about

35

milk after infancy toilet training try waiting. 'I was over toilet-trained, my mother toilet-trained my brother and me early and as a result we are obsessive, I keep things in my office in neat little piles.' 'Do you dear?' said his wife, 'I certainly hadn't noticed.' I remarked that I was all for tradition, especially ones that I had heard Thailand used to have: feeding white elephants from the bare breasts of young women. What I really had in mind, of course, was myself, hanging onto one of my wife's breasts while my son hung on the other.

Meanwhile I went for long car rides, checked in at some motel, got pissed for several days in succession until the limousine caught up with me and the chauffeur lifted me into the car, up to the briefing room, where the old man paced the walled-in room. For reasons best known to himself he liked to keep a fire burning in the fireplace even in hot weather and compensated for the attendant heat by turning up the air-conditioning. He kept lighting and re-lighting huge cigars, offering me one, knowing I'd refuse. Refuse the terms, conditions, decisions. Our plans have been overtaken by events it seems look isn't it about time you...

Sweat ran down my spine, chest, crevices, as it had likewise done in that oval office. But now I was surrounded by endless desert and I started seeing
unmarked springs
avocado groves
fertile islands
mammoth lakes
sheer walls of symmetrical blue grey basaltic columns
crystal-clear hot springs
6 packs of fridged beer
641,000 acres of lakestrewn land
a sea life housed in 13 large glass tanks with perforated seals and prostrate mermaids

20 to 30 feet high snowdrifts in 65 underground air-
conditioned rooms with swimmingpools (heart-shaped)
surrounded by white marble statuary
conical 115-foot towers under water
aquatic birds in ceramic tile combination baths
3 barless bear pits
an outdoor hippopotamus pool with a 24 hour room Food
& Valet Service with Guest controlled Built-in Vanity
mirror, ideal for Group Grope functions
Comfort stations and mercury vapour lamps atop 27
towers overlooking an animated relief map
pergolas and spring-fed lily pools
illuminated wet walkways.

Towering above these I saw her as in many slides. One
of her in the pink brocade swimsuit and green rimmed,
green tinted sunglasses. She sat beside the pool, a
huge floral sunshade decorated the sky above her. She
waited for her parents' guests. The lawn had been
duly sprayed with green paint over the bare patches. I
remembered that day seeing her from the bathroom
window, and as usual felt roused by her from such
distance. I was under the shower, surrounded by the
hi-fi, bookshelves, television, weighing machine and
the two sun-lamps fixed above the shaving mirror.
The thought then was: my greatest accomplishment
while I remain here may be my mere survival. Cool
it. Shoot first, think and ask questions afterwards.

I passed some tourists dun-buggying in their
Bermuda gear, and noticed then the gas was running
out. Perhaps this had also happened to them, maybe
they hadn't even reached the freeway. I could pass
them, wave cheerfully, while she stretched out in
semi-consciousness in the back seat, while he
trudged through the desert. Want some help? I'd call
out as my Chevy churned up dust in his sweaty puffy
face. And later I'd dutifully visit her shrine along
with all the others: the wee Kirk o' the Heather

reproduction of the church where Annie Laurie
worshipped. The reproduction of the church where Gray
wrote his Elegy in a Country Churchyard. And attend
while there the hourly lecture on The Last Supper. The
Hall of the Crucifixion, measuring 45 by 195 feet. Note
that visitors must remain during the showing, and pass
out as the lecturer got to the 180th part of Christ's
body. No. Give me the USC any day, it looks like a
Missouri Farmer's vision of Shangri-la. Basically the
USC is a mail-order meditation society. No problem
is too complex or trivial for Silent Unity. Stock-
brokers and the Yale man 'phone for prosperity
thoughts. Intrigued Charles tried meditating on his
withering hip and soon affirmed it back to normal.
Yodonna from Globe, Ariz., testifies that 'I received
fillings in my teeth'. ('Why not let God be YOUR
dentist'). Yodonna also testifies that she prayed with
Oklahoma's Oral Robert and got new spinal disks. Some
of the faithful create their own prosperity banks,
cardboard containers, into which aspirants can drop
pictures of things they want
Gooney birds
intentions of a potential enemy
Jane Fonda
a mock mental collapse
contagion in Minneapolis
an arch apostle of the money supply theory
otherthrow of Puppy Palaces
a vacuum cleaner that's noiseless
Protesters are encouraged to repeat short prayers
like 'I am free praise God I am free the prospering
power of God pours out on me and fills my every
need.' Phone lines into the Room of Light are open
round the clock for anyone in need of instant
inspiration and 'reverse the charges'. Balloons, large
elastic vibrators, tambourines, gold hand cream
and other stimuli are passed around for noncerebral
pleasure. 'That's what religion should be,' says a

Beverly Hills grandmother, 'a kind of available, constant, impersonal love.' Advance men have prepared the way 'You got to promise God, and you got to keep the promise. If you want him to lift your pain, to make you whole, to bring you joy, you got to have faith. Faith. And faith is to vow and pay.' But the real power still rested with the bishop in his diocesan quarters, marble floors, red plush draperies, gold-framed loveseats ('a throw-back to monastery cow stalls'). As we ate I saw him pitch a handful of pebbles down on one of the trees. Instantly the sound of an organ wafted up from the garden, and our host explained 'That's my orchestra. The boys keep napping.' Within this Roman villa, young ladies who will be dazzlers if they ever grow up, are placed consecutively head to toes, would reach all the way to Heaven, which is precisely what they represent. On good nights, the faithful and curious stream through.

The gauge hovered over the E. My mouth made of sand. Whole body seemed a sinking dune buggying itself back, forward from the steering wheel. I saw their car off to the right. But I could see no sign of either my X-wife or her lover. Hiding perhaps in the back, the gun loaded, waiting, ready to leap out. The bloody ending as inevitable as the climax of a Greek tragedy. So they would want. The episode could hardly be bettered: the vaporous, honey-coloured scene as my body writhed to earth in a quarter-time choreography of death. A mythical legendary, balletic ending. The tone of the scene shifts in a split second as the bloodied victim attempts to aim his gun, forgetting it is unloaded. After the affair has been discreetly seen to, they trade in the Buick one afternoon for the same model in another colour, borrowing her father's chauffeur to trundle it through the desert until it had accumulated the early mileage. She might come out in hives, her usual accessory to any crisis, and her mother applies glycerine furiously over her daughter's body, collaborating that Men are Monsters, just beasts that they act like babies, and you just try getting a man to take the pill... For several nights she'd cry in the king-sized bed. Or would it be the Queen size? Half a foot wider, almost half a foot longer. A welcome and luxurious 20% more room to stretch and sprawl. Separate individual coils. Coils that aren't wired together, so they don't sag together. Shift a hip. Dig in a shoulder. Roll this way and that. Exclusive individual coils give every inch of the body the firm, flexible support it needs. Each sleeper gets single-bed comfort in this new Queen-sized bed. No collisions. Togetherness is optional.

Ah yes that bed. And others larger, smaller, narrow, wide, where we played out our experiments. I the dwarf, she the Queen. Sister. I the President, whose favourite plaything is a ball of twine which I shed with hair on the furniture and visitors. The go-go cage outside the doors has shapely dancers, who do not actually appear sans apparel, they wear various coverings to simulate the impression. Waitresses clad in bikini bottoms and pasties serve noon-time Bloody Marys and roast-beef sandwiches. We even dressed up for these scenes, and had all the necessary equipment:

Prostitute	half-bra of shimmering satin the sensational lift supported the under bust urging her up and out and leaving her excitingly bare but fully supported.
Lesbian	a penis-aid to assist, non-toxic, flesh-like material with LIFE-LIKE VEINS
Nymphet	grease-resistant - easy to clean. Soft. Pliable.

| Flagellist | a raised clitoral stimulator. Comes in three colours. EBONY. BROWN. FLESH-COLOUR. |

We arrived at a stage when even words were unnecessary. A record collection when each piece of music fulfilled the appropriate background. Head full of musical organs. Feet scaled the walls. Strips of light placed between the toes. Her ears were sitars blown by my carved mouth. Sitting in the shower, spinning fantasies onto her back as she leaned over the bathtub, plucking at myself, the feathers of geese and quail from thigh to neck. Upsidedown. From right to left. From left to right. Turning her over in the flat of my dreams. Her mother waved from a desert tower. Her father lay on a bundle of stocks and shares directing the family traffic through glass stairways. I stripped bananas and thrust them up her, half way, ate the rest, poured sour cream over her and buried my tongue, fingers in the remaining pink areas. Her feet followed the trail of foxprints in snow. Markings of spiders along the orifices. Patterning of fine ridges which characterize the skin of palmar surfaces of the hands and the soles of the New World monkeys. Basically these games were an attempt to make sure something exciting happened every day. The list of attractions became formidable, both in length and diversity. She had a definite flair for restless inventive rhythms like an unending conflict between God and the devil, who slips in and out of her movements like a familiar visitor. She believed in salvation - of a secular variety and searched for it insistently. Often she'd adjourn into the bathroom and lock the door. God knows what she did in there, I couldn't even look through the keyhole she had stuffed newspaper in it. So I carried out the fantasies on my own on the king-sized bed. More than 100 life-sized figures in 35 scenes. Hand and footprints imprinted in a coral like crust deposited by waters of an ancient sea.

Thoughts now encounter shelves of projecting ideals from these enormous arcs of nostalgia thrown high in the air rising 20 feet and spanning 50 feet in the arc. A large depression whose floor is scarred by numerous ideals.

In my sophomore year I was considered a clean-cut boy, born of a sturdy woman whose mother once killed 45 Indians with a broom handle. Weaned on moonshine liquor when I was three years old. He can walk like an ox, run like a fox, swim like an eel and make love like a mad bull. At fourteen I was permitted by girls to go so far if I was on a leash, crated, or otherwise physically restricted at all times. My youth contained a series of leap-frog bridges. Blind closets, trapdoors and secret passageways. A huge overshot redwood wheel. At seventeen a self-guided trail explained an immeasurable earth fault. I joined the navy.

A world all its own... lean, long lines of supersonic jets, the dark flanks of nuclear submarines, the vast bulks of aircraft carriers. A sound of bosun's whistle and running feet - a look of readiness. For a moment, enter the world of the ever-alert. I became like a trained whale who performed frequently in the tank. A 2 billion dollar mothball fleet a persistent dream, from which I dived out of into a simulated ocean abode where divers made several regular trips a day to feed me by hand. Where I made it with octopi, Hawaiian fish, sea horses and other unusual creatures, and joined in the performances of porpoises playing basketball, baseball and other games. Penguins paraded near the main entrance of sleep. I noticed a tendency in the other men after two or three weeks to display pictures of grossly unattractive women as their pin-ups. These plus the subnormal daily activities made the content of dreams so dense that the only life within them consisted of small briny shrimp and the pupae of the ephyda fly. I began then to organise a free-form dimensional equipment in the shape of a bucket. Digging below the surface the continuous bucket line operated 24 hours a day, except on July 4th and December 25th, and I viewed the dredge from foreign lands.

After leaving this sea circus I made a retreat within myself, an inner pilgrimage, a road to Damascus, a mechanical Mount of Olives, Hamlet and the spectre of General Motors. Secretly I was a creative warlord, ready to lead tatterdemalion innocents into a blood-letting orgy.

Enter Intersputnik, cohesive design, luring away beyond conventions Superchief of Information. I believed in play now cry later. A day in the life of a political activist: seduced and abandoned by a nympho in home movie. Credit risk, observatory in the sky, stair to heaven. Scornful of weakness, new landfalls, lunar boomerangs for birth control. I had a new surge for a tired old idiom the seedbed of a psychic revolution. Omar offered compassion and peace, the Crusaders slew and prayed. I would form a new administration manning the Pentagon, an array of able technicians, a nest of torturers nailed down and stand up to Big Brother obsessed with dogs and calculated cruelty at the Stockyards. I decided monuments just didn't pay the arsenal of resistance, the Politicians' preacher, the right and duty to follow one's conscience in the corner. The Mix of the Fix data for domestic tranquility surveying dribbles of food, purple geese and other fighting fauna, and a severe case of angst in Europe Society's spoiled darlings. I heard the death rattle of an encircled nation, and saw the enchantments of a luminous land, Glory to God in beaten organ pipes, years of frugality and a doctor's bill. Someday I'll get you Red Baron.

My conscience began to show. I was no longer competitive. I grew my hair and sometimes a beard. I developed the reputation of being a difficult person. The hour of doubt is heart-rending; nothing is nothing, everything is everything, one's faith wavers and idols gleam with tempting splendour. Even when you're walking, lying in bed, sitting in lotus position, taking a shower, punching your Giant Life-Like Karate Practice Dummy, or writing a crostic sonnet to a diaphanous creature, you may prefer, somewhere deep down inside you, small-capacity engines with double overhead camshafts, direct steering, gearboxes with a short lever you have to manipulate in your palm at critical moments, and fast, precise heel-and-toeing even if you're afraid you won't do it right. In fact I arrived at that time in life when there's difficulty finding the reality of the reflection rather than the reflection of the reality. I thought in terms of cartoons, each frame changing. I wore bold-textured high-riding slipons and appeared to others all mood and pauses and long stretches of languor.

Numerous trails afforded access to 45 improved and hundreds of unimproved areas. Moving sidewalks through sub-tropical forests marked by blue and gold signs picturing an albatross. No sooner was I out of the navy than I realised I was still eligible for the draft. I heard the voice of authority, set jaw, practically bald hands on hips 'You mean you're refusing to step forward?'. Above the singing of This is My Country by the Mormon Tabernacle Choir many shouted Good Luck and there were friendly signs held up. But they were soon rocks and they'll aim for the command post first. Every week I got a letter from my mother telling me not to take any chances. I contented myself with daylight puffs of Pall Malls on the roof, and anyway I really didn't want to go outside

at night because it would mean missing my favourite
radio shows
The Lone Superman
The Green Hornet
The Shadow of Lux Man in motion overland on and under
the seas, through the air and voids.

Man's wanderlust conquering time. Who's helping to
increase his mobility? The R.D. (Re-frocked Diplomat);
the M.A. (Mythmaker Allies); D.Gs. (dependent
Generals); the N.I.M.H. (National Institute of Mental
Health); the D.S.I.A. (Diaper Service Industry
Association); S.D.S.A. (State Department Security
Agent); and HEW. My personal feelings on this flight
in many ways centred on the hardware files that
reached into every family; eager pegs waiting to be
plugged into some 1,500 holes. In my spare time I
enrolled at the University and took courses in
body surfing   howling at the moon   fencing with Styro-
psycho-drama group encounter   foam foils
sandal making rock music   sensitivity training
tree climbing the coming holocaust radical politics
                                    Swedish massage.

To cope with neuroses and nuisances there was a
centre offering help after bad trips, and a generation-
gap mediation service (for parents who can't handle
their kids and for kids who can't handle their parents).
Only one thing was missing: a significant portion of the
male population issued an impassioned plea for their
mother. All I longed for was a home, a comfort in
common with every luxury hotel. Complete freedom
from pests, the Founding Fathers and the National
Idea. Hallo we have in our hands the name of one so-
called anti-communist patriot who applied for a visa to
Red Russia this year, plus 300 Micky Mouse sweat-
shirts in various sizes, together with a Clarias
Batrachus (Asian walking-catfish) also a private
collection of pubic hairs gathered from various

celebrities. Will you Herr Reichspresident entrust Herr Hitler with the remains of your loved ones? Yes yes said President Von Hindenburg Yes indeed? And in the Waldorf room Horatio Hump did a little jig.

I soon realised that you don't use a gun on an IBM computer you just pull the plug out. Emerging from the Army with snail-like deliberation I began seeking a comfortable marriage. At that time I was given to mustard-coloured suits, green-on-green shirts and a travelling entourage of verbal audacity 'I make the Esso tiger look like a possum.' 'I make George Wallace sound like little Lord Fauntleroy with laryngitis.' The biggest question, of course, was whether my psyche could completely adapt to the situation. The experience was suspenseful, fearful, gut-gripping but with this one there was a big difference - a deep visceral understanding that here was an act that might ultimately guarantee my survival.

Again I pictured her face. The face with unshaved eyebrows, the tiny blonde natural lashes, the large nose, dimples at the mouth corners, one up, one slightly down when smiling a certain smile, not one cultivated in front of the mirror. The other face becoming her mother's. Lines in downward movement, eyes clinging precariously to rouged sunken skin, suspended over men by a clever cantilever system, while she manipulated situations equipped with a hydraulic mechanism to tilt an entire floor. Marked rings indicated the many important events which occurred during her husband's investments, and when his shares fell, as likewise his mood, and nothing was right, she'd take off in the Buick sometimes in the middle of the night, with her inflatable plastic man instead of the chauffeur. Blowing up her 6ft tall 46-inch-chested escort, propping him up in the seat beside her.

46

The night I took a walk around the replica of a south sea island, planning a means of escape. He left one day in a private railroad car that was detached from a Union Pacific train in the desert outside the city. Carried on a stretcher, his face covered. A more likely version is that the man on the stretcher was a decoy to distract attention from the lanky rather melancholy-looking individual who ambled in a few yards behind. I was just planning to get across onto the island when my mother-in-law drove up, screamed something at me. Certainly her husband looked strange, I thought. Perhaps she had finally killed him. At first I felt out of it, caught up among the fuzz all turned on at the start of a murder enquiry. But on studying the tooth marks on the body I felt I might be of some use. The marks, were, after all, plain enough to identify the person who had done the biting.

As I walked towards the car, she bent towards him, he became a small effigy she pushed into the glove compartment. I had fought the vulture before. I knew her style. Maybe she wanted me to rape her. Wanting that all the time, to be hauled out of her tower, gagged, bound, stripped, dragged across rocks, tied to a tree and beaten. There was a kind of flowering dullness about her, a boredom in rosy bloom, though at times she had a sequinned sexuality, slightly parted lips, petulantly cajoling baby voice, silvery teased and teasing hair, but she belonged to another age. She asked me if I'd like to go to the movies. We went. Later we went on to a casino. No clocks to distract, no doors or windows that might reveal the position of sun or moon. So I had no idea how long I watched and raked in the money for her. Then we went on to some nightclub, where we perched with other diners on observation platforms of fake railway cars. Waiters dressed in French sailor suits pranced among the tables, while, over the loud-speakers Tiny Tim sang

Tip Toe Through the Tulips.

While here she told me she had once hoped to become a nun but was rejected after three futile attempts to adjust to convent life. In fact, she said, she had to cope with the hulking crush of one nun whose hostility became infatuation. She survived flea bits and amulets in the mattress, and bypassed such leading questions as whether shaving under the arms costs a woman her sexual powers. She defended her own obsession with Gothic eccentricity in plain terms. It was most certainly Christ-haunted. She had, of course, masochistic longings, apparently allowing some wino to abduct her. 'He did not purposely harm me in any way,' she said, with a rather sad smile, 'other than the fear, the tension, and the hardship of being in the woods, and being away from my family.' At night when he slept, she was chained by her neck to a tree. She showed me the marks, touching them with her stiletto nails. In fact they looked more like scratches than scars from a chain.

Exhausted we drove back, but before entering the grounds she told me to stop the car. Her hands fumbled over me. She brought my fingers on to jagged walls, formations of eroded red sandstone. Footprints of a giant sloth, bones of mastodons. Be careful. Look out. Get back. Get out. Be cautious. Get ready. Drop gently. She was large, wet, her massive legs over the steering wheel, breathing heavily as she had over dice, faro, chuckaluck, roulette. She had curious formations shaped like shields or palettes. A lump of sage brush. How could I have got out of that one? I realized I had no chain with me, not even a rope. I kept my eyes closed and saw a deep-blue inland sea with a sharp pyramid-like island rising 475 feet above the lake's surface and she became a breeding ground for more than 10,000 huge white pelicans.

That's how most of my escapes were defeated.
Summoned by my father-in-law the following morning,
and over several highballs I was put through the works.
'Look when people come to my house they follow my
ritual,' he explained, 'and when I go to their house I
follow their ritual - it's that simple and as for last
night well I don't think that it would be ethical for me
to discuss what happened at this time.' He didn't look
at me, but continued doodling with one of his
unbreakable ballpoint pens, and there was a cautious,
hold-your-breath optimism as he waited perhaps for
me to confess what had gone on between his wife and
myself. I remained silent. He went on 'Look I worked
to get this place...my gal has had the best education
possible...her mother and I have worked ourselves...
it looks like you're determined to throw our family
into anarchy and drown it in iniquity and violence
however I can assure you that force can be contained
we have the power to strike back if need be and to
prevail.' I fixed another highball and looked out into
the rose garden at the 8,000 bushes displayed.
Azaleas, orchids, rhododendrons, begonias, fuchsias.

A stay at his No. 2 home, a palm-fringed winter
retreat, on an acre of land fronting a lily pond, was
arranged. That lasted a week, his daughter grew
bored, had hysterics, developed hayfever, and came
out in hives, and had nightmares of bears carrying
her off into the mountains.

One of the high points of a vacation for some people
comes after returning home. It's when they can see
for the first time their camera handiwork snap-shots,
through which they will re-live their trip over and over
again. A reel-by-reel search for reality. The best
angle may be from a lily pond. Can film be truth at
24 times a second? As soon as you start shooting
something it becomes something else. You've got to
stay on top the tiger or you'll end up inside. Will you

permit us to film your death?

For some reason when we returned to the No. 1 home
she didn't tell her parents I had threatened her with a
gun, nor my attempt at suicide in the pond. Love
shines from pictures of quiet moments and family
mile-stones. 'I'll never forget the way you looked that
night on some even curlers are cute and here we are
in let's see where was that honey...?'

I saw them suddenly at the bottom of a large dune, she
was making up her face. Soon they were in hot pursuit
of their quarry. 'I want that man get him,' she shouted
as I drove past, raising sand in their faces. To die
like a God! No I can't chicken out at a time like this.
Just before reaching the freeway the gas ran out. I
slid under the car as they turned the corner. They
seemed to be having an argument. I heard some slapping
going on, who was hitting who I couldn't see. Soon the
car heaved above me. They had got into my Chevy!
'Look let's wait here - he'll be back - gone to pick up
some gas - why don't we...' I heard him saying. She
began crying. The car heaved a little more, followed
by silence.

Ordinarily he's just a quiet guy in a dark suit who
comes around once in a while to talk. Shy. Retiring.
Not one of your pushy types. But suddenly emergency
strikes. Burglars in your bedroom. Garage fire
bubbling the paint on your new Cadillac. Hurricane
Zena heading straight for your chicken farm. You
call for help. In a flash, he becomes the Man of
Steel and flies to your side. To protect your rights and
fight your battles, and give you good counsel as long
as you need it.

What were they up to - making it in my car? Or had he
had enough? So simple to strangle her quietly here,
leave her in my Chevy - what more evidence? The
blonde liked fun and gaiety; and she ended up a cold

corpse in the desert. I crawled out and ran across
into their Buick. I noticed she had already got out,
completely surrounded by desert, she sat high on one
side of a broad saddle between bare broken peaks.
Josua-trees stretched in all directions. He appeared
in a semi-conscious state, blood poured down one side
of his small-town boyish face. I always knew her false
nails were filled with poison - like mother like daughter.

I started the car up and drove past. She ran shouting,
waving after me. As the lad grew older, he learned to
his delight that he could hurdle skyscrapers, leap an
eighth of a mile, raise tremendous weights, run faster
than a streamline train and nothing less than a
bursting shell could penetrate his skin. But a woman.
Wonderwoman. How could the Man of Steel not
succumb to her? She had been accused of lesbianism,
fetishism and sadism, at least in our games, but
really she was just an ordinary goddess who wanted
to marry and settle down. Beautiful as Aphrodite,
wise as Athena, swifter than Mercury, stronger than
Hercules. And the mole 2 inches northwest of her
navel. This suddenly remembered as I watched her
flying down the highway, blonde hair a mass of gold
cupids circling her head. Her pale fragility and the
thought of that mole, nearly had me. I slowed down,
but as her face approached it somehow reduced the
level of tragedy to mere silliness and I pressed hard
on the gas, until she became a pale distant desert
figure. Liberty and Independence or Death in Pursuit
of it.

Homicide can be fun and we today can build a great
cathedral of the spirit, each of us raising it one stone
at a time, as he reached out to his neighbour across
the pollution-spewing stacks in Pittsburgh. Meanwhile
the Secretary of Housing relaxes by riding horseback,
playing golf, and jogging. His complicated electronic
rigs suggest the possibility of communication between

men and mice. 'You have to give the other his turn
and you give signals at what he says to show that he
is having his turn. You must also refrain from saying
anything that really matters to you as a human being
as it would be regarded as an embarrassing intimacy.'
The sessions take place in a barren room with a
minimum of props. The usual musical accompaniment
is the pounding of drums, their agony is instantly
recorded on a Rube Goldbergian array of lie-detector
equipment attached to nearby flora. It could be that
the President plans to alter the machinery so gently
and quietly that most folks will hardly know what
happened. Are you suffering from Muru? The
inability to walk, loss of speech, difficulty in
swallowing? You get it from eating human brains.

I soon realized I had the inability to drive any further.
I needed food, lodgings. Above all a place I could
drive right in without getting out of the car. Park in
a covered parking area, place my luggage on a
super-market-style dolly, and go directly to my room.
Sleep. Then a night life cosmopolitan and mature. But
it was the usual blood-drained formica, noisy, fridged
air-conditioned room. Too cold if I switched on the
conditioner, too hot when off. I lay on the under-sized
Queen bed and watched the tube. The everywhere
check, if you push-me pull-you, all wired for a trance
in the wilderness. It will be there through good and
bad in the empty hours, just when you need it. Sounds
made visible, a missile's white clicking teeth, a
dolphin's voice-prints pick arsonist and Nasser on
phone. The sound 'ga' helps make a conviction. A
mental patient relaxes. 'Ah' says the President, the
big-sky man hemmed in 'every man his own furnace'.
Hottest prospect is a fat male genius says a post-
graduate historian. The issue is as old as freedom,
'In my day we all had faces.' Mere millionaires don't
count now. Monsters of Moonport, the biggest

discovery since Columbus. The frenzy of youth manipulated by the viewers' communication that puzzles, excites and involves. Work a risk, change the channel with real foes on every side looking for a wedge, while cavorting cops aim low, clicking shutters, cut and faint. Ban the Germ Mediterranean style towards the doomsday bug. No withering seal limbs, upsidedown biology. We can see you on 15 Caribbean islands caught in the crossfire.

Good morning you just made a decision about your stocks now to sell the capitalists on people, rigged subsidies tackling IBM towards currency change. Coercing, exploiting the problems abroad, proceeding with fewer missed beats than ever. Do robots live forever? The clear rigid mind of Mr. X launches warheads from orbit. The computer gets the answer. On-off language feeds in the data, model train tracks route to solution, his warts an' all. Ultra-sensitive microphones in the sound-proof chamber. The view is global and includes two dream visits on the coral route. Who was the guy who said the sky's the limit? The Nation's insecurity makes it more difficult. Inter-marriage is the only long-term solution, National pride prolongs it. They could create special insured plans of mutual funds, pay Balance in event of death guarantee, net amount of investment on tenth anniversary. But 1 out of 60 is a shoplifter. It's the season for thievery. A mother steals crayons, a drug addict lifts a sweater from a respectable housewife. The oppressors and keepers of a covenant. A father's fury foiled, so who's in charge? If you agree with us that our Withdrawal Plan has been a good way to have fun then send for details about hits and misses with goats and sheep.

I switched off the boob tube. But then decided a truly perfect duologue would be two TV sets tuned in and facing each other. One tube ran the ad intact, the other performed surgery on the figure's silhouetted breast. Their desire for variety was certainly not objectionable. Charlotte let her gown fall to her waist, her breasts covered by two 3-inch TV sets. 'By using TV as a bra the most intimate belonging of a human being, we try to humanize the technology.' Voters learn about upheavals everywhere on TV. Fear is contagious. But as the mayor-elect, he is not primarily concerned. He must figure out how to run a city with a population of 490,000. He promises supporters that he would consult widely before making any decisions. But he stressed: 'My chief adviser is going to be God, and don't you forget it.' A mother of six confided that she had chosen green for posters because 'God loves green, or he wouldn't have made so many things green. And I wanted to show that God was on our side.' And at an outdoor barbecue Prince Philip grills the steaks. His wife sticks a finger in and helps herself to a lick 'oily', she says as her horse is served his carrots on a linen-covered tray. And at a ghetto garden the First Lady cooed over a farmer's collard greens and admitted that if she lived there 'I would be out every day with my little hoe - gardening is my favourite hobby.' She encouraged teenage weight lifters near the Watts ghetto with a little of her own body. 'I really want to work. I don't want just to lend my name.' 'I think this is the answer to our problems,' she said, as she offered her hand to hesitant black men 'I'm not afraid of anything, these children are really learning to enjoy life.'

Suddenly her face became my X-wife's, all my X-wives appeared in scene after scene, commercial after commercial. Greenish-white skin grew in clusters, sucking me in, down. Good travelling companions anywhere would include a long dark robe, bedroom slippers and sufficient lingerie of fabrics that require little or no ironing. Not bad - though for stimulating

a sense of rare expectation there is the Instruction
Manual on free-floating levity: a man squeezes a tiny
woman out of a tube of toothpaste. Another discovered
blood leaking from miniscule teeth marks under his
watch band.

Again I switched the tube off. Tried to sleep. A couple,
stoned by the sounds they made, moved in next door.
Laughter. Shrieks. Water splashing. A combination
shower. That's what I needed. A travelling companion,
without robe or slippers, perhaps just wearing
transparent lingerie. Then what kind of alter-ego
would I switch to - I might become a man with special
extra dimension - coolness under fire. Though he
sputters and sparks like a loose high voltage wire
across a highway, there is a direction to his excess
energy. Being in his presence is a cross between
electrocution and contact high. In any event his
invulnerable confidence in his mode of dress, based
as it is on a solid foundation of unshakeable lies, has
given him a kind of unearthly glamour. He took to
wearing all at one time an avocado cap, avocado
turtleneck, avocado sports jacket, avocado socks,
avocado sneakers and avocado lovebeads with orange
streaks. He also had a wardrobe consisting entirely
of lemon-coloured jump suits. In the curiously lit
world he might have seemed 34 or even 28 years old,
depending on the shade, the time of day or how close
he was sitting to the bar lamp. Slight and round-
shouldered, who flinched, smiled a crooked private
grin and sometimes even seemed to walk on a slant.
Or better still a rejected candidate for the priesthood
who is elected Pope, who is a hipster-hood acting on
market fever, hyponotized by growth, squeezing out
the last juice from a London Accountant and his pet
otter. With camera and sound equipment he tracks
down a group of New England Bible salesmen. He
quickly laid to rest any illusion that he coddles

himself. He hoofs it everywhere. His curiosity about bedsprings, long snouts, shower nozzles and kitchen steam tables is insatiable. When he heads for the airport he jingles with good luck charms: a bassinet, silver bowl and spoon he used as a child, masks and feather hangings, his World War II dog tags and a charm in the shape of a naked lady. As for being elected Pope he admits 'I don't have the shape and face for this thing - my face is like a Halloween mask.' The demon lover swaggers before a mirror; a clown peers back. His involuntary memory provides him with a series of erotic flashbacks. During one session he bounces up and down on a TV remote control. He nourishes fantasies of a future in Miami. 'The confrontation of people's stomachs,' he said, 'is more important than any other confrontation.' When he discovers that his followers are all government spies, that his vatican papers are no longer secret, and that his power is nil, he decides that since he has been politically dead for years, he may as well relax and retire. When asked about his papal experience he confided 'I have found that rigid teaching is simply impossible of observance by many faithful and generous spouses, and I cannot believe that God binds men to impossible standards. Adam and Eve after all can be a Mexican hippie and his girl turning on to some groovy apples in the grass and these are peepshows into paradise - they are a cry of beauty created with skill and affection. Don't take them for granted. They will soon be gone from our world.' But a few have been more outspoken. Said one young man: 'the wire will be snapped off, the plaster will break, and the carnation will give off its perfume again.'

I had broken into a cold sweat. Where were they now? Perhaps she had been picked up by a truck driver. The fuzz. They'd bust me for god knows what: robbery, assault, rape, murder. Laughter behind me rose.

Creaks, squeaks from, no doubt, an extra long king size bed. I turned the tube on again. My second wife's face stared out at me.

Picturesque diversity. Varied recreation. Games of chance, topnotch entertainment. Eerie lovers before me. Colourful clothes and food. Positions I never thought myself capable of. She had taken up Karate. I arrived in her black belt phase. A blonde Bomber who sent her men flipping over furniture, including the bed, with one twitch of her mighty hips. As her bumpy bruised knuckles attested, she could be equally menacing with an uppercut 'I never can keep a long nail' she moaned. She was also a militant hedonist in constant search of the best that can be eaten, drunk and fucked or otherwise savoured. She liked arranging happenings. It was at one of these we met. Shoulder high in dough I was finding the whole scene pretty draggy. The happening was a 3-ring pretzelrama with an 8-foot mound of every imaginable kind of bread. People were leaping right in, while others sawed, hammered and kneaded the dough all around, and threw half-baked rolls at those who had sunk into the dough, all to the amplified noises of bread baking.

Of course she was extremely good at aiming, three rolls hit me on the nose, and I swore that when out I would... I was furious, at the yeasty mixture on my new tan corduroy suit that didn't zipper or button down front but sort of stuck together from neck to navel like masking tape. When I did get out we fell into each other's arms and stuck together. Her first words were: 'The activist response to the fear of death is not to prolong existing life but to try to achieve rebirth.' I was turned on by her immediately. At that time I was going through a kind of salvation search. I even think I had a pocket sized edition of the I Ching on me at the Happening. Also I had never heard a woman talk to me like she did. I had up until meeting

her the fundamental male concept of females: that
they were wet, shrill, hysterical, formless, irrational
and deciduous. Soft too. She had a softness even though
she was physically stronger than me. Her daily routine
included a 45-minute session of isometrics and a
workout with the dumbells: 'I've got to keep in good
shape - it kills me that my insurance policy forbids
bobsledding though I don't mind its ruling out getting
into the prize ring and skiing.' I watched these
sessions once, as the performance somehow proved
to be so sexless that I didn't even get one mild tingle
from the acres of flesh that paraded about as thrillingly
as a bathtub of jello. On the other score, however,
when she wrestled with other women I had to leave in
my embarrassment of a continual hard-on.

She was, in fact, the woman every man thought was
just an ordinary goddess who wanted to marry, have
half a dozen kids, who was really a lesbian, fetishist
and a sadist, who set up cageless quarters and unusual
compounds for her lovers. She had one big hangup
at the beginning of our affair. She told me she had
never experienced a full orgasm. Even a $40 session
with an Oriental head-shrinker had failed in
discovering why she had never achieved the ultimate
satisfaction a woman should have. She said she'd
marry any man who could achieve this. Well naturally
I tried my best. The first time we made love it was
like entering a self-supporting garden city combining
bucolic charm with big-city nerve. He had come to town
with an excellent reputation for competence and with
excellent personal relationships. He was sharp, wry, an
eminently respectable fellow with a light but persuasive
touch. Then why such an elemental blunder when in
bed with such a woman? She said I was doing it with
my mind. I blamed her for telling me her hangup. So
for weeks were both hungup. She frigid. I impotent.
She mentioned something about impotence being

already formed by the tenth week of intra-uterine life. She was always ready with some home-spun psychology to make matters even worse, and liked analysing my dreams. Soon I learned it best not to relate these to her; I was psychotic enough without the extra neuroses she delighted in handing out for me to deal with.

On her birthday she received a long Victorian night-robe sent by her mother, which she immediately threw in the garbage. Later half stoned I lifted it out, and told her to at least try it on. She refused, but suggested I put myself in it. I did, and giggling, we made it on the kitchen floor, with the garbage clinging to the robe. She achieved the ultimate satisfaction. Or so she told me. About three times she said. Two weeks later we were married, and went off on our honeymoon, the robe carefully packed, which I was destined to wear every night, sometimes in the afternoons. When she began having lovers after three months of marriage with me, I wondered if they were given the robe treatment also. I inspected the garment often enough, but never found any evidence. Maybe she had bought similar ones. I searched through her wardrobes, closets, no sign. Other things I came across. Relics of past and present admirers. Photos of herself in Karate costume lifting another woman on her back. Dim photos of what looked like some black mass orgy. I recognised her body on the altar. I was curious and strangely excited. When I asked her about it she immediately arranged for a black mass to be held at our place that night, and introduced me to 'their leader'. He was sleepy-eyed, scraggle-bearded, and went by the name of Nightripper, and it was rumoured he was also called Mystic Murderer. 'Most black magic,' he drawled 'is a hustle to get fast money.' He handed out to our small gathering (mainly women) potions such as Van Van rub and John-the-Conqueror

GOD BLESS OUR HOME

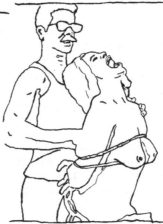

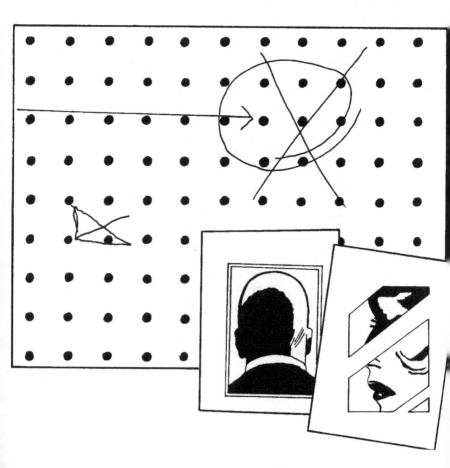

wash 'for the jealous "boss-fix jam".' When asked about things he'd seen, he chuckled 'Once, after a rain in steamy St. Louis Cemetery I glimpsed the ghost of a nineteenth-century sorceress and what happened there was the height of depravity,' he said, smiling through his war-painted face, feather shako and wriggling his silvered toenails. 'I intend to go back to New Orleans to flush her out of my cells.' He had apparently waged a vendetta against Eleanor Roosevelt, whom he dismissed as 'La Boca Granda' (the big mouth), and termed the President a 'feeble-minded Führer'. He had been accused of everything from coddling criminals, handcuffing the police to approving hard-core pornography and banishing God from schools. He struck me as a complete phoney, but what curiously enough irritated me more was that my wife, and the majority of women who surrounded him were completely in awe of him. What made it worse was that I felt sure he had been to bed with every one of them. He looked a flagellist, in fact capable of every perversion possible.

Not to be outdone I suggested we all strip and rub one anothers' bodies with some very special oil I happened to have. My wife immediately muttered 'sacrilege', and abruptly turned away from me for the rest of the evening. Partly because of her attitude and my own position in all this I started looking around at the other women. There wasn't really much choice. I chose about the youngest, a girl who still had the air of highschool around her. I really wasn't turned on by her, however, she seemed to respond amazingly quickly in the candle-lit room to my hands which at first I only dared put through her long dark hair. I whispered that we should go into another room. But as we were sidling out of the door, my wife, who lay naked on the altar, incense it seemed wafting from her body, called out 'if you want to do anything do it here only don't bug my trip.'

I had the feeling that other than the potions Nightripper
had handed out he had also passed around something
else. The scene resembled a Bosch vision of hell.
Some of the women were staring, some were unusually
happy, some were sick, others were screaming, and
some said the walls were moving. These days if one
escapes being hijacked in an airplane, mugged in the
street, or sniped at by a man gone berserk, one
apparently still runs the risk of getting accidentally
zonked by the hors d'oeuvres at a friendly neighbourhood cocktail party. As soon as I thought this I began
hallucinating, and ultimately freaked out, overturning
the altar, calling Nightripper my motherfucking
father. Apparently everyone soon left, except the
girl, who my wife asked to stay, hoping between them
they could bring me through. I remember there was
a point when I didn't want to come down, but remain
on an edge that appeared to touch upon a very thin
line between life and death, and such power! I felt I
was capable of anything, by merely putting my hand
out things would fall or rise. I was Satan with God as
my servant.

The following day was a letdown, yet I felt
extraordinarily calm. The girl remained, there was
a recognition between the three of us. Obviously my
wife was turned on by her, or more possibly turned on
by the attraction of competition. So for 6 months we
shared her, or rather they shared me. There was
very little jealousy, except when I might make love
to one without the other being there. As long as they
both had their turn then things were relatively clear
and right between us. That was, now I think back on it
all, one of the happiest times in my life. I really
did feel like a God. Both women were so different.
Their moods, gestures, language fascinated me. One
or the other calling from the bedroom, and there
they would be lying on the bed waiting for he-man

body strength powered with
520 muscles
18$\frac{1}{2}$ inch big arms, powerful to land a knock-out blow
fast
52 inch Heroic chest housing tireless lungs for
endurance in work, sports, and women
a broadmuscle packed back
wonder-wide super man shoulders tapering to a slim
punch-proof waist
big muscular forearms
a steel grip
legs with marathon endurance. I was at their beck and
call.

Over one of the women for the second time just 2$\frac{1}{2}$
hours after beginning. I would move slowly for five
minutes then accelerate fast enough to tear myself
loose from the other's embrace. Rising Phoenix-like
above my own exhaust flames. O.K. I shouted hang
onto your hair I'm going to turn you upsidedown and
when it gets pretty draggy doing it that way we do it
this way. I gestured at the ceiling. The first time the
three of us got into bed I missed badly on the first
two attempts then waited about 20 minutes, I began my
approach and pulled up. Finally I braced myself and
rushed through the silence. I had no drive I didn't
manage a really powerful take-off all night. It doesn't
happen very many times in a man's life that he
consciously and deliberately faces death. Perhaps the
most nerve-racking part of it all I felt then would
come when I was ordered to lift-off from one and land
on the other. Too short a climax would, of course,
toss me into a trajectory and send me smashing back
into an orbit alone unable to reach either myself or
the women. Often as I climbed over them both I
thought hold it Mac one false step could be your last.
You must make a quick decision. That strange feeling
in your guts is back as you think this is a scene I'll

never forget and you may even stay the rest of your life but you see your hand rise and hear your voice cry Move Out. ATTACK! Both women I felt had secretly been taking a boxing course through the mails. But often the scenes were wild and beautiful.

A fluid dance, and all our limbs flowing into, out, through, until I had no idea whose hands, breast, leg I touched, or was touched by. Time seemed no longer time of real life but a hugely amplified present. When fantasy has the weight of fact; and fact has the metaphoric potential of fantasy. The experience existed only within its own context, on its own terms. A certain rhythm, a nervous montage. Trips not on established trails. A series of spectacular switch-backs. Domes and carvings, arches and flying buttresses. Subterranean desert life. I stretched out along a floor of inland seas. Their bodies merged into a river flowing upsidedown. Afternoon skin became bronze, red, gold and purple. An ever-changing panorama of delicately coloured formations. Scenic, narrow, wide, winding, mountainous. Forest areas composed mostly of slightly rolling terrain. I remained as long as I could in my lookout tower which afforded this magnificent view of the surrounding areas. As I sat there in the half dark their bodies became strangely natural rock sculptures of animals, miniature cities, cathedrals and temples. A riot of pink, red and orange, white, grey and cream. Here and there splashes of lavender, pale yellow or brown appeared unexpectedly. The girl, who was destined, of course, to be my third wife, had an amazing way of composing her limbs in triangles. Leg upon leg, arm on arm, leg on arm, she had a really beautiful body, with the kind of skin that is transparent, and becomes more so after making love. Often after the three of us had exhausted ourselves, I would doze off and return perhaps to more innocent days.

The tale my grandmother was fond of relating, while
she cradled me in her rockingchair lap. The tale
of the witch woman who spins off her skin on the
spinning wheel. In seconds I was back where I lived
as a kid. The work my father used to do. My trip to
school. The games we played. Exercise giving us a
good appetite. How we spent the afternoons. How
everything has changed now. The special tasks
distributed among brothers and sisters. My grandmother. The morning meal. A small amount of
porridge on the floor and the whole world listening.
The thought. The grandfather. A cousin, bald, always
old. A house. A happiness I would not care to reproduce.
Undefinable radical childhood sensation. A mood
created. Recreated in which irony invariably plays a
part.

The moods the three of us had constantly changed from
excitement
terror
violence
embarrassment
idealism
seduction
rapture to despair and finally a kind of utopian domestic
hygiene. At times a leaping dance in the belly of a
monstrous fish. No earth, only a watery expanse. No
sun in this watery world. We experimented and kept
experimenting until we arrived it seemed at exactly
what we wanted. Until it was one neatly controlled
vista after another. Everything was nice, pat and
predictable. It was all too much. It was like dying and
going to heaven and deciding we really didn't like it
there. The chief problem was psychological not
physiological. There had been the failure to infuse
'community consciousness' - the absence of boredom.
The women started taking sides against me. Rejected
products are not confiscated and may be shipped to

points outside the area by recognized common carriers if the owner desires. It was never clear finally who rejected who. The arguments, the fights became constructed. Structured. They accused me of evasion. What was I evading? I became confused and when I'm confused I'm very confused. The problem I soon discovered was that my wife had grown restless sharing me with another woman, and the other woman had fallen in love with me but also loved my wife, and my wife had fallen in love with Nightripper.

There I was feeling fat and happy in the middle of the road and then blap whamp whamp whomp sok thud whak zapp whokk thudd bam zowie I got pushed on all sides. Pushed to the outer reaches of the seas inhabited by monsters about to eat me up or burn me with their fiery breaths. Recalling it all now I wonder why I hadn't split then and there as soon as I knew what the deal was. But I was trying, after all, to act civilized, like they said they wanted. I lost weight, became pale, twitchy through the constant vigilance needed to negotiate such hairpin curves. Unaware at the time that a trip into such an area should never be attempted without adequate preparation and equipment. My mind a multiple dome structure housed dark grey jumbled thoughts, desires, needs. The situation had seemed so ideal. Two women and myself, why couldn't it go happily on? I had even devised the project of having a memorial coliseum built for the three of us. Yes a Coliseum which would feature a hyperbolic paraboloid roof, inflatable partitions, and an acoustically balanced sound system. Memory lives on... Forever. Lovely, colourful Memory Stone Memorials are famous for their beauty, permanence, craftsmanship and Double Guarantee Certificate.

In all that happened I guess there were various signs, omens that I never took into account at the time, for I .thought I understood the nature of the difficulty that came up, even though I could not precisely ascribe the difficulty to a certain failure. I felt the procedure would be one where I had procedurally implemented methods of circumventing the problem and felt sure that should it occur I had procedures that would be able to cancel the kind of problem we might have got in. Under intensive pressure I summoned them to breakfast and delicately exhorted them to 'toe the line' and told them that they must decide in accord with their consciences: 'If you don't see your way clear to going along, I won't hold it against you.' The whole time I faced them the simple thought of leaving the planetary cradle stirred me. If they weren't going to leave then I would. The delay wasn't strategy the decision was just put off and put off and put off. The original theory, of course, held that to keep both philosophical sides of the house happy while disagreeing with them on an issue every now and then I had to throw something in they could chew on. I realised that a strong move in the physical arena would have done much to solve the wounds they received on other issues. The theory could have worked. But in practice I seemed to have vacillated between indecision and a tendency to rash action. At times I simply walked out without indicating anything. I was aware that I must be willing to fight and to lose sometimes if I wanted to lead. There had been the failure to provide the requisite leadership from the outset, a related series of bumbles, errors and miscalculations. My one and only defence soon became silence. This caused all manner of happenings, major subdivisions, violent hysterics. And it was hard to remain on the inside of the road I built for myself that afforded such ambiguous security.

I felt alone, bewildered, paranoid. So much so that soon I found myself aimlessly drifting in what seemed a large limestone sinkhole. Again I thought of splitting and told them so. Then split man split, they screamed. I've made my pitch here I shouted back. But the pitch failed, and I vowed to press on the situation - it was plainly moribund. I thought of the migrations of loons, grebes, glossy godwits, ring-billed gulls and black terns, and envied their flights and cycles. There I was on foot down a precipitous trail, equipped with high power binoculars, for any moment I suspected the women to leave before I did. At least for one of them to go. Both remained. They apparently awaited my decision. A choice. The problem was I had an abundance of decisions. All of them prone, many in fragments. I couldn't whip them but where could I run to? He had power, speed, but unfortunately he was what we would term a playboy. Somewhere in my rear consciousness there was a reconstructed gallows, and in another area a hand-hewn wooden cross of considerable size.

In dreams at the time I was forever pursued, and attempting the most amazing death-defying battles ever fought. In one dream both women had bald-headed lovers with pubic hair around their mouths. They changed into Oriental women I came across in a room, both menstruating at the same time. Another dream haunted me for days. I seemed to be kneeling in a small ice-cave, looking out on an extinct volcano dominating surrounding fields of cinda dunes, lava squeeze-ups, spatten cones and inactive hot-springs, and a mountain eternally in the rays of the setting sun. Dark at the base, the volcano became rosy, then shaded to various tones of yellow. On top of this stood my wife. I shouted for her to come down. She disappeared. There were loopholes in the cave walls that gave the aspect of a fortress. Then the sand dunes shifted, and the silicified bones of prehistoric creatures sprang up and danced towards the ice-cave where I was surrounded by well-preserved bodies. Living replicas, duplicated of all the women I had ever known, or had wanted to know. I attempted touching them but as soon as I did they became fossil heads, breasts, fossilized cunts. All the dreams came close to the emotional catharsis of tragedy, or approached something even rarer: the catharsis of outrageous comedy.

Most of the dreams were pretty wild, so much so I think my second wife grew jealous of them. Later, much later, after that divorce, I learned she felt I wasn't wild enough. Her first lover apparently left her his private flat designed for orgies, complete with floor mirrors and elaborate camera setup for making movies of all the fun. Copy of Krafft-Ebing in hand she went through all the paces, developing a real yen for the Aristotelian perversion. Her next lover was a sadistic leather fetishist, chained her to the bed, locked her in the attic. The next was a Chinese anthropologist who went around at parties biting the knees of faculty wives. Her dreams, I suppose, were obvious, according to her shrink she had destructive tendencies, which meant she wanted to destroy her parents, plus all the men she went to bed with. I well understood the desire to kill her mother, whose visits were composed of a series of wisecracks and verbal castration, prepared constantly for fights to be staged throughout the day and night.

> Lizzie Borden took an axe
> and gave her mother forty whacks;
> When she saw what she had done
> She gave her father forty-one.

Her mother was proud of their blue-bloodied ancestory. 'They weren't on the Mayflower they met it,' she was fond of saying, and went on about some great-grandfather who lay buried in a graveyard containing the graves of 180 notorious characters, many of whom died with their boots on in the settlement of violent

disputes.

Her mother also believed in ghosts and told us that
there was one in our apartment. 'This is where you
hear the apparition - you hear it coming down pfft
here.' She pointed somewhere at the top of the stairs.
Her Siamese cat Twinky apparently was also psychically
sensitive, 'for whenever an apparition appears Twinky's
fur stands on end.' And for some reason this blue-
bloodied mother was an expert on fleas, explaining to
me one day about the jigger flea being the sexual
marvel of the animal kingdom, comprising very little
but genitalia, and that Sweden's Queen Christina was
fond of hunting them with a 4-inch miniature cannon.
I wondered if she also had a similar machine.

That's what I needed right now, only not a 4-inch
cannon but something that would at least deafen the
couple right behind my bed. They seemed intent on
wrecking their motel room, either that or making it
all over the place. Things, metallic, fell against walls,
doors, windows. Accompanied by screams. My God
that scream I recognized! They had obviously seen
their Buick parked outside. Or perhaps not. Pure
coincidence. The nearest motel on route. Maybe they
really didn't have any idea I was the other side of
their wall! This is serious - very grave... it does not
lend itself to any emotional irresponsibility... the
consequences are too horrible. Don't let this once-in-
a-lifetime opportunity get away from you. Face them
both, demand what they are up to.

Down through the ages, the green-eyed demon of
jealousy has wrought death to those who have fallen
under its spell. Once again, the spirit of possessiveness
sets a trap that lured an innocent man and woman into
a drama which ended in murder! Naked and Dead in
Room 1011. Clues were few as Police set out to find
the woman's Sadistic Killer. He was a cruel killer

with ice water in his veins, knowing neither compassion nor the pangs of conscience. He was an expert marksman, and he killed friend and foe alike.

A dynamic erection party if need be. A rather splendid parabolic menace that coheres. An almost biblical fervour bubbling away beneath the ambiguities. There must come a day when my capacity for accepting injustice has to be arrived at, the point of maximum endurance, the counter-measures taken once that limit has been exceeded. And Christ when my first wife is stoned there aren't any limits to her acting out the sexpot temptress for all she's worth, with a let's-have-fun look in her eyes. A taut-bone-bare throbber for a manufactured joy scene. A fabulous collection of eye-catching breathtaking pulse-warming boudoir 'play clothes' that dare to be different and dramatic, more exquisitely beautiful than anything you've ever dreamed possible. Created to tease and please - for the siren, sophisticate or young at heart. Dressed in her Frou-Frou. French coquettes adore this shocking new brief - it's so naughty, gay, youthful! A next-to-nothing frill of lace, neatly elasticized to hold the sheer nylon lace crotch in place.

Ideally she would want golden peanut shells to sail away, perfume in the faucets, floors of coloured tissue paper. Purr and fur. A thousand whipped cream pies in the face with open mouth, a bed shaped like a banana split
velvet rugs
leather chairs
tables shaped like turkeys
cranberry candles
Rococo atmosphere
diamond dust mirrors
camel's hair wallpaper
gold-plated doorknobs
adjustable muzack

Beethoven in the front and rock in the back with the
offknob on her navel. A million sex thrills for breakfast
and nothing makes you fat. Despite the auspices and
intentions, no dry bare-bones, but a lovely lyrical
motion. Invariance under a transformation. The first
part built entirely around the symmetries of reflection
and rotation and their combinations.

I had always rationalized that if there was any ambiguity
between her wants and my actions, non-actions, it
finally worked through a highly cultivated naivete and
economy of means. It was often enough to make me
want to mutilate myself, shit in my pants and love it,
drown happily in my own shit. Often I eclipsed her
stoned sentiments with a blinding flash of pure,
driving primitive power. Which, of course, she wanted
all the time, and the whole scene transferred us into
cutesy animals contained within a semi-sadistic chase
format. Then it came, like a mile high tidal wave at
my back, breathing, quivering, waiting to suck me
up, to charge and destroy, as though nameless forces
of destruction hovered just outside, with a losing
battle fought against strange things with wings. A
crawling armoured skinned, fire-spitting, man-eating
monster that preys on any helpless enemy. She'd play
at being the compulsive fellatrice. But that can be
stopped with courage and daring. If you provoke it,
leading it on and on, dodging its fiery breath, decoying
it into a snare, springing the attack of anti-spider-
woman devices, it all depends on you - you're the
'live bait' in this one.

I wondered at what stage she was in right now behind
the wall with him; sitting, no doubt, blonde and
spangled in eternity, both slut and angel, pure and
corrupt the cynosure of both spirit and brute carnality.
As for myself well I may as well have been in a Sonoran
arboreal desert with memories handled like auto-
erotic symbols. Incestuous masturbation between

brother/sister; uncle/niece; father/daughter. As well as a case of initiation involving mother and son.

How often I had wished mine had. Your mother loves you and your father admires you and your relatives like the way you wear your hair. It could have been a rejuvenating process for my mother, living out in the sticks as we did that many years. A system of canals and large storage reservoirs. Irrigating the formerly arid region. She might have become a radioactive hot spring. A bath-house plunge, or an entrance into Russian vapour baths. The records of fantasies on this route are so clear that even the untrained eye and ear recognize them. This was particularly so when I was sixteen and she stopped tucking me up in bed, that was when the moraines were enormous. The descent on my own into sleep became extremely diverse, with sheer drops of 2,000 and 3,000 feet into rock bound gorges, carpeted with hairy patches and wildflowers sprouted from overhanging breasts. I doubt if I ever forgave mother for marrying again, someone 15 years younger than herself, and only a couple of years older than myself. A mother-fixated used car salesman; an ex-surf, ex-track, ex-movie actor, ex-married guy who viewed the world through habitually squinted eyes. Skittering about like a bespectacled magpie, a sprite of the cashbox, who somehow thought mother was well off, and out to explore the outer reaches of eros. When younger, his mother insisted that in a wig and dress he was a dead ringer for Shirley Temple. Amongst his belongings I came across the following interview.

Interviewer: Don't you ever wake up in the middle of the night and realize you haven't done anything that is really artistic?

'Shirley': So that's what the people above are doing.

Interviewer: What do the kids want? Hollywood

today is terrorized by the mercurial tastes of restless children.

'Shirley': Film makers are mostly babes in the woods nobody is what he's supposed to be.

Interviewer: The way out then is through rebellion?

'Shirley': Work for 50 years, contemplate for a hundred, be born again - or thawed - and, as a child, but supremely wise, learn how the new world goes.

Interviewer: Your thesis is persuasive but it's only a cut above a five-minute dissertation on the Oedipus complex.

'Shirley': Do you think anybody who knows what he's doin' would give you good information for a nickel?

Interviewer: Once you are a superstar, there are two choices open to you: You can become a bore or a monster.

'Shirley': Dolphins also are pompous moralizers. They have not only learned to read and speak English, they have learned to write novels, although not very well.

Interviewer: Let's talk about your bosom kit it consists of a cleavage delineator to tip blush right?

'Shirley': People are striking out for simplistic approaches. Any guy who talks about some of the real problems isn't in fashion today.

Interviewer: Never one to do things the easy way I understand you prepared for your role by broad-casting that you were the eleventh-generation descendant of a Mayflower immigrant - to paraphrase Mark Twain: 'Lead us into temptation. . . it builds strong character'. Would you agree with that?

'Shirley': The days of busy-bodies and social cancers

with boots up to their knees and collars up to their ears are hopefully numbered.

Interviewer: Which leads us to the generation gap...

'Shirley': My father and I have gotten much closer lately at least we talk to each other on the 'phone every Christmas.

Interviewer: As Charles Lamb observed 'Credulity is the man's weakness, but the child's strength.' It is rumoured you are writing an autobiography - is this correct?

'Shirley': In a way yes but it's a book out of quotes that show the moviemen to be innocent of cruelty or dirty dealing, but guilty of venality and grossness.

Interviewer: Is this the reason why 20th Century Fox fired you?

'Shirley': Groundless reports - Fox supplied the ghostwriter.

Interviewer: It's also been rumoured you are making a film about sexual excesses of ancient Rome?

'Shirley': I might one day but at the moment I'm re-making Snow White with the idea that the mother is a Wicked Witch of the West who really wanted a little girl and has a boy instead so she dresses him in drag, who in turn meets up with the seven dwarfs for convivial auto-eroticism, they induct him as a new member and he turns out to be turned on only by the mental image of the Lone Ranger.

Interviewer: You, of course, play Snow White?

'Shirley': Oh no I'm the wicked queen and it's not going to be one of your quasi-skin flicks shown in a peepshow in Times square.

Interviewer: Where, of course, your last film was shown.

'Shirley': The past is part of the present, just as the future is. We exist in time. That's what I learned in Monte Carlo. I learned how to manage the present.

Interviewer: For generations stars have pondered the problem of how to grow old gracefully, toupees, corsets, heavy makeup, gauze filters and lawsuits seem part of that last memorable personal appearance, how do you feel about growing old?

'Shirley': God will give me an instant mutation and ship me back to this planet as an embryo-without-portfolio. Salvation will be through God, not through science, even if the movie casts the Maker as a slab.

I soon discovered that my step-father, in fact, was a seemingly intrepid liberator of mankind who's cringingly adept at saving his own skin, a born false Messiah. Even now I can almost smell him and his ALL-PURPOSE LOTION; see his shower soap on a cord, packed in a redwood box - that brings out the Devil in a man. Sometimes, some days, things just don't go right. That day my mother came back from the Beauty Parlour, all dolled up, looking a freak, and said 'Son I've finally found the man who can knock your poor dad right out of my head and that's why I'm shooting the works new hairdo the whole bit I'm pulling out all stops to dazzle this guy - you just wait you'll get on you'll see how great he is.' I suspected they had met via a computer.

As soon as he turned up on the scene our family life from then on turned from a semicircular urn of intimacy, a kind of womb with seats where mother and I had nuzzled together so comfortably, into battle scenes played in a refrigerator. He arrived that first time in a 1911 Buick Bug. And later I heard them carrying out their monstrous crime. The following day he slipped a sparkler on her finger. And that was that. I went about learning how to become a fearless self-defence fighter overpowering any bully twice my size. He was a weakling while I was an Anabas that could travel overland, breathe in and out of water, climb trees. I shaped up my body into the lean, sleek hard-as-a-rock condition demanded of spacemen. Ready and able to do things in a big way - with the same kind of long-lasting stamina, the same tiger-quick response that astronauts need to stand up under the gruelling demands of space programmes. I knew I could no longer impose a preferred solution, but must seek to evoke it. Her marriage at first, in fact, cost me considerable sleep and two notches in my belt.

They took me on their mile-high City skyline honey-moon. A neon muddle of motels, restaurants, souvenir shops and pizza stands clustered around amusement parks. A Pigeon Dance & Squirrel Crawl, people dressed as animals scampered among assembled pigeons and squirrels of the park. An Egg Roll event featuring hundreds of Chinese egg rolls rolled on a clipped lawn. A troll Booth stationed under a bridge where several ugly gnomes declaimed the Endless Relay ahead. Oriental bells, whistling paper birds and musicians hanging in trees.

The dark, scowling observer went unhindered and discovered notes they wrote each other: I AM LOSING MY INAUTHENTIC SELF I am becoming Thou, True, Good & Beautiful Immutable Love. It's been an intoxicating experience yesterday, today and undoubtedly tomorrow. I continually felt like the small boy who didn't get an invite to the party and just wrote his own and went anyway. Mother took to wearing clothes that made her somehow look like a truckdriver

in drag. A blue chiffon, midriffied rhinestone-zipped
pair of pajamas; a Grecian toga with chains around
the bosom, and a shocking pink crotch-high dress.
She also took a slimming course. Checkpoints on one
of those lanky model's topographical map include a
depressing flat chest (in some cases it would even
seem the highest prints above sea level are the veins
on her neck or the end of the clavicle) a curved spine,
hips that can be flung into a grandstand without being
provocative, no thighs to speak of, and skinny legs
and arms that can be bent into pretzels or used as
tooth picks at cocktail parties. Did mother really want
to be like that? Fortunately the diet didn't seem to
make that much difference, though her face became
definitely not to the manner born, or the image I had
of her, round, ringleted, wide-eyed and smiling a
pretender's smile. 'Drink', she'd say, waving a multi-
ringed hand towards the waiter's belly button. While
my step-father dressed in egg yolk front - pleated
pants and skinny red knit top came on as if he was the
essential western man, fearin'. God but no one else.
Tough to men and kind to wimmin, slow to anger but
duck behind the bar when he got mad, for he had a
gun and a word that never failed.

I watched them from an enclosed lounge with high-
powered telescopes
from a replica of an ancient Greek temple
behind an electric fountain with its 125 combinations
a mountain-rimmed valley
a mainstreet shoot-em-up and hanging
watched as they held hands
as they walked into, out of an old mission church
a jail
stage depot
trading post
saloon
morgue

a boom town of tents, shacks, saloons and dancehalls.
A storied stronghold of kooks, cults and lacy little old
ladies in tennis shoes. A night's crocodile hunting.
After you've made your kill, the guide will skin the
crocodile for you and you can arrange to have the hide
tanned at a cost of $4 per foot. Often they wanted to
be just together in their 'togetherness', so I was
hustled off to lectures and discussions on such topics
as Heightening One's Sensitivity to Other Peoples'
Signals. The Causes and Effects of Possessiveness &
Jealousy in Love Relationships. Solving the Problem
of Sexual Lack in an Oversexed Society. Self-Defeating
Behaviour - How to Counteract It by Living
Humanistically. I counteracted mother's behaviour by
coming on as an anti-hero, showing human feet of
clay. But I wasn't this for long. For some reason,
while watching a buffalo herd roaming some land
adjacent to a park, mother slapped new hubbie's face.
That's when I stepped in, determined to flatten him
like he was a peanut shell. Punched as full of holes
as a telephone dial. But she stood between us, and
looked kind of small, old, wild and remote where only
wild palms are found. I suggested we all go for a
drink. Then he gave it me: 'I wouldn't have a drink with
you if you were the last person on earth and I'll tell
you something else you just watch your goddamned
step when you get in my area you just step out of line
once more son and I'll bust your arse so fast you won't
know what trouble is.' Butler, baseball pitcher, disc
jockey, movie actor, cop - I knew he'd held down all
these jobs at one time or another. And all dear mother
said was: 'Don't you think, honey, you're overacting
a bit?' I decided the only thing to do was to keep
moving and hitting the enemy in order to assure my
own safety. Keep him off balance, subject him to
constant pressure so that he could build up enough
energy for new offensives. Always to be stepping on
the enemy's toes and maybe do a little kneeing and

gauging at the same time. So I bought some snoop-equipment. A television camera 8 inches long and an inch in diameter that can be hidden in a victim's house or office.

A radio transmitter as small as a cigarette lighter that can be heard half a mile away.

A listening device smaller than a quarter that can pick up conversation, through a standard hotel-room door.

A tiny electronically activated camera that uses special film to take pictures in the dark.

And a Spikemike that could be stuck into a wall and I could hear their corny conversation the other side.

When a snooper can't get close enough to use his tiny microphones, he can use a large circular microphone that looks like a space-age gun and will pick up conversations 300 yards away.

I knew that things couldn't go on much longer as they were going, and the prospect of a climax to the whole affair had its own deadly fascination; the most downbeats of endings can be thrilling if the beat booms big enough. It doesn't take much to get the spirit of apocalypse these days. My own fantasies at that time centred on population engulfment DDT and oil spills spoiling all seven seas, and Melvin Laird on the morning of Armageddon, still insisting that the ABM will strengthen our hand at the bargaining table.

We moved on, into an area that was reported to have 3,000 hours of sunshine a year. That week it rained non-stop. A region I well remember of gaunt juniper-dotted mountains sloping away to bare red rocks. I studied the town's early days recorded in a series of eight oil murals. I also studied my step-father's movements from a Corinthian-style structure in the form of a Greek cross. It was 272 feet above ground and afforded a magnificent vista. A vista of factories for manufacture of tires and rubber accessories

porcelain
serums
fishing equipment
fine instruments
saddlery
and incubators. These, in fact, were my step-father's
latest ideas while on the honeymoon. He'd start up the
old man's factory again, and maybe spring some new
ones. Manufacturing
refrigerators
freezers
dishwashers
air conditioners
blowers & exhausts
steel and aluminium
porcelainized building panels
automotive & casket hardware
aluminium extrusions
and various dies.
Then all his dreams, and hers too, could be realized:
a Ritzy home. This turned out to be a child's idea of
a castle, sandblasted concrete with nine turretted
towers glowing like imprisoned sunlight, glass having
succumbed to stone. And behind the facade, the stairways, would be cascades of red-orange carpeting.
Low ceilings dimpled with lights embedded in them
like flat moons, with throwaway nooks and crannies
having no function except 'to delight' his eye. And as
they sit on the balcony ignoring the plastic ivy,
delighting in the magnificent grounds, the swimming
pool with its reflection of rising moon, and the
emerging stars above, while his wife attempts to
quieten her husband down, 'darling, precious love
shut up I don't want to hear your yapping I want to look
at the beauty God has given us - when by the way was
the last time you really looked at the Milky Way?'

We hate to seem ostentatious but the next sentence will

be about his Purdey custom-made shotgun, or how he just had his grandfather's ring 're-florentined'. I, meanwhile, dreamed of a place consisting of four cultivated acres isolated from the nearest road by a two day pack trip. Raising my own vegetables, fish, shoot game with flintlock rifles, I'd build and bore myself. Make my own clothes, mostly out of deerskin, and read Hardy, Tolstoy, Gogol, Emerson and The Wall Street Journal. And, of course, spend a lot of time simply sitting around, or poking into the wilderness to see what things looked like. I would only go into this wilderness after I'd beaten up my step-father. But inevitably like Jesse James was shot in the back, Billy the Kid died as he entered a darkened room, Wild Bill Hickok was shot from behind while playing poker, I would be the victim that had no chance to defend myself. And after that well I'd like to have been stuffed and mounted in a museum wearing my Goth suit, carrying all my guns and knives and on my forehead would be stamped 'Be Prepared'.

Mother was certainly not prepared, nor had the stamina for her husband's seven cities of Cibola. With her background of having been raised in sprawling cowtowns she was quite happy to see them both, myself included, living a peaceful life in some apartment with sun deck, ocean view, a nearby Sultan's lounge, and Golden Palm Coffee garden. She listened to his plans, dreams, ideas. Attempting to be attentive while he sat there with great mounds of information on his knee, so much that the brochures, catalogues insurance policies fell on the floor, and he scrambled for them. There was about him the cautious cunning of a longhorn feelin', smellin', and knowin': 'I'd rather be slow and right than smart and dead,' he was fond of saying, like 'you can play in a pigpen and you are going to get mud on you.' Yes why not why don't we get a nice house, a large estate,' mother would say, sighing. And I

remembered her telling me of her life with the old
man, recalling one night during the great depression
when funds had dropped so low that she had a feeling
of actual desperation clutching at her. 'But your poor
father was never put off his stride, "The Lord will
provide," he said "Let us just keep on serving Him
and trusting He will give us fresh insights and ideas
which we will turn into workable plans." Well then you
came along,' she said, 'and the years passed yet we
never missed a meal and we had nice homes with all
the necessities and some of the extra comforts, he
was right indeed the Lord has taken care of us.'

I wondered if she still knelt and prayed to the good
Lord before climbing into a stranger's arms. Perhaps
she prayed secretly, silently while he went on about
the place he'd have built, where they could plant a
3-mile avenue of alternate pines and oaks leading to
the house. Have their cars ornamented with gold, and
be awakened each morning with sprays of perfume. I
know that whenever she started out with any fantasies
of her own he would suddenly cool it. And for a few
hours he'd say nothing. But few of the cool-off
programmes had the size or scope to achieve anything
like a lasting solution. In every case the purpose, for
myself at least, was to get through that summer and
buy the time needed to mount an all-out assault on the
root problems. The main one being my step-father.
I left pamphlets around on the breakfast table, aware
that he was increasingly paranoid about his bald
patch spreading.
Losing Your Hair?
The breakthrough in the study of baldness and hair loss
has been discovered: At last, baldness may be
prevented without the use of ointments or massages.
Explosive new theory claims that hair loss is not
primarily a problem based on heredity or hormone
deficiencies, but a common biological malfunction

84

which may be easily and inexpensively corrected. The Vaginal-Aid inserts into the 'users' vagina and allows the woman to experience the effect of the VIBRATION UNIT. The VAGINAL AID is comprised of a SAFE Non-Toxic, soft plastic tube that is sufficiently rigid for easy insertion and a SPECIAL Electro-Magnetic VIBRATOR UNIT
Battery operated and comes apart easily for cleaning.
The Prosthetic Penis Aid
Allows the MAN to engage in prolonged acts of intercourse even when ERECTION IS LOST due to
EJACULATION
IMPOTENCY
OBESITY

But these high-voltage jolts of shock therapy apparently only turned him on all the more. I even suspected he wrote for the equipment, out of sheer perverse curiosity. I heard every move, every moan my mother made from my room next to theirs, as I rolled, twisted on the massage bed until I turned into some kind of vibrator freak. The light knob by the bath door had a rheostat controlling the six bulbs which ring the great mirror. The more you turn, the brighter the lights go, and then back down, delicately adjusting to the amount of truth you can abide in.

I even disguised my voice and 'phoned them up. The anonymous caller was making telephone wires hum, if not burn, with his particular brand of vocal garbage. To what extent can an individual practice psychological Mate Selection on his own? A tangled knot of rope, a pile of dirt, and himself nude, but covered with mineral oil, moving slowly while clasped in the arms of a lovely female dancer. All in all it was a situation thick with peril constitutional as well as personal.

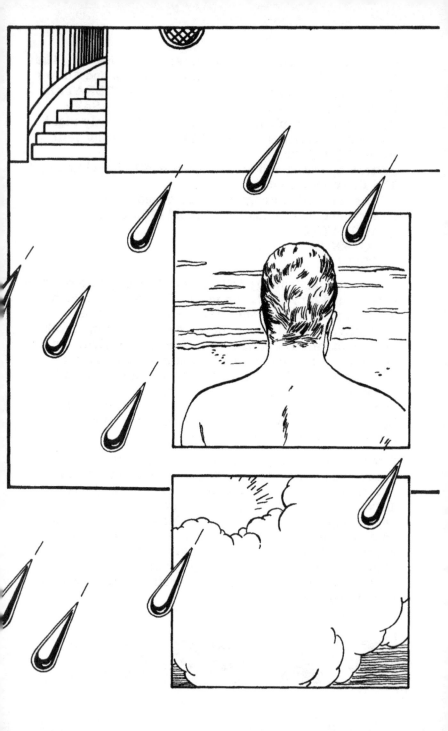

Product of Evasions?

It's always a relief to have not heard from you for a long time it means that there is no crisis and I will survive another week.

Love Mother

P.S. If you feel as bad as you looked in the photo you last sent me you should come home for convalescence.
P.P.S. Enclose a letter from your step-father - he

refuses to tell me what it's all about. But whatever it is Fie on you! St. Patrick you know is alive and well in the breasts of all his faithful. Beware! What he did to the snakes, he can do to you too.

Words From the Temple

I was amazed, shocked and mystified by your actions, let's face it - one of the first rules in life that a child learns is that you don't take something that isn't yours.

May God have mercy on your soul.

Yours Dad

The Personal Element

Your recent letter is as welcome as a breath of fresh air used to be, even though most of it was taken up with informing us that half the population is afflicted with hair follicle parasites. I'm certainly not going to have little mites running all over my face so I'm going to sleep in future with the light on. Anyway halitosis, b.o. iron-poor blood, nagging back-ache and some others were becoming a bit shopworn. Well take care, you know letters ain't my easy bag, but I'm always happy to get one from you. By the way Dad is getting along fine with his nose-job. Did I tell you he got some of his large nose removed from an expert doctor in Dallas - now he has a quite respectable nose.

Love Mother

P.S. Re your answer to my suggestion 'Food stamps are more trouble than they're worth' most of us have to exert ourselves to some extent to get food for our tables - some of us even have jobs. Anyway I know you're not underfed, aged or handicapped.

Something to refresh the spirit

I don't have anything to say this week.

Love Dad

Hail to the Hero

I do not mean to reproach you, or even to give you the
impression that I think you'd care if I did. But it appears
to me that you have obviously graduated to the oldest
juvenile delinquent in the nation. I would like to point
out that if mankind didn't have some mammoth project
to direct its attention toward, civilization would
decline. At present the only project that you have for
relief of boredom, your mother informs me, is
marriage, and as you make your giant leap into that I
really feel you should have firmer footing than a
garbage dump. This recent event makes two things
painfully clear. The first is that no matter how artfully
the new you double-talks, the old you manages to trip
up and assert itself, reverting like an adolescent does
when he sucks his thumb. We have never all agreed
with your decisions, however, most of us accepted
them because your mother strongly believes that you
represent 'The epitome of honour among men...'
Disillusionment sets in when we find that the cream
of the crop is really only curdled milk.

Frankly I have had a long-standing grudge against the
Daughters of the Republic of Texas (at the age of
4 I was asked to leave the Alamo as my pair of
cowboy boots were 'desecrating the shrine' with their
noise). However I'm sure your wife will prove to be
a good wife (she'll have to be if the marriage lasts)
and I wish you luck.

Love Dad

Love Thine Enemy

While the rest of the family are feeling rage,
frustration and indignation at your actions I am
feeling a more hurting emotion - that of disappointment.
I am stunned to realize, even in this cynical age, that
you have such utter disdain and contempt for the basic
intelligence of the family you have joined. Your reflex
action towards self-perpetuation following crisis only
underscores your lack of humanism and moral courage.

How well I remember your impassioned albeit ill-
advised charge of 'irresponsible' which was levelled
at me when I married again. Jesus of Nazareth was
not deterred by the cross. Where are your priorities?

Love Mother

Try a Little Tenderness

Darling come home. Everything straightened out.
Need and love you.

Your wife always

Startling Discovery

What the hell's the matter with you don't you know
girls are made of sugar and spice and all that's
nice?

Your sugar-bunny

One Adolf Too Many?

My daughter vindictive? Hell no! She merely told a
measure of truth about a person both selfish and
spoiled. Truth does have a way of coming out. Your
decision was ill-advised in the first place and a tragic

waste in the second. You have finally paid a personal price for feeding at the trough of ego. But in the final analysis we have paid for this fiasco.

It is incredible that as astute as you are supposed to be, you haven't realised that your silence is your loudest accuser and with so many of us in on the secret, either conscience or cupidity will force the complete story into the open.

The old man

Lead Us Into Temptation

You said we have a long way to go. I've made a modest start. I feel good. You helped. Please oh please come home.

Your honeydove wife always

P.S. I consider our marriage still holds. It was hardly what you'd call the greatest since creation, but it was a first, kind of.

I'm Not Yelling!

If you haven't improved enough by now to cope with your problems, let's face it, you never will.

Love Mother

Antidote for Cynicism

Now that your marriage bubble has burst, has it been just a bubble? Wasn't it a highly organized spectacular, glistening and eye-catching enough to serve as a short-cut to the better living club but lacking in the elements of maturity and substance. Our family would do well to place our fortunes in the hands of those who have won their spurs each step of the way.

Love Dad

From Dream to Nightmare

So now you have discovered that if I drop the verb
'to be' from my language I would become more honest
and less dramatic (Your letter of the 23rd). Very
interesting. You are obviously getting along almost
entirely without 'to be', but this does not seem to
have brought about a notable increase in honesty and
open-mindedness. I realize that noble rhetoric is no
guarantee of noble results, but when you came into
our family I had high hopes of raising a great cathedral
of the spirit and forging a family of open doors, open
hearts, open minds.

The old man

Here Are the Villians

I thought your letter was slightly less penetrating
than the mouse that attempted to fertilize the elephant.

Love your X-honeydove

More By Less

You're gonna build, no matter how you destroy. You're
gonna teach love, no matter who you hurt. You're
gonna be useful by being useless. You're showing
commitment by not being committed. You're gonna
lead a new social order without a leader. You're gonna
reject materialism no matter how much you have to
sponge off me. You're showing a new morality, no
matter how immoral you have to be to prove it. You
are going to show a new purpose by having no purpose.

You want to create new rules of no rules. You reject
technology by using my microphone, my car, my
booze, my prepared foods. You want to be nonproductive
on my production. Now I understand why I don't
understand.

The old man

The Durable Matriarch

You say 'I feel the tragedy of our breakup'. That's
what I'll have to live with. But what I don't have to
live with are the whispers and innuendoes and
falsehoods. Oh, but you do, the slings and arrows of
outrageous fortune are one of the facts of life, just
as are slanted communication media, and to say that
you don't have to live with them points sharply to
lack of emotional and mental maturity.

There is a good deal of clutter here, whether you need
your mother to wipe your nose with all due respect to
your mother, isn't it possible that it is not your nose
which needs her attention, but your perspective.

Your X-wife

That'll Be The Day

Brothers Grimm, move over. You have been topped.

The old man

All In The Family

This insult shall not go unavenged. It was bad enough
when my brother, my sister and my cousin Philomena
witnessed your intolerable tantrums, but this time
you've really gone too far.

Dad

93

Well-Deserved Epitaph

You have stated that if you had done or said anything
amiss that you desired us to think it was your infirmity.
My wife and daughter hearing this cried 'Alas, good
soul!' and forgave him with all their hearts, but
there's no heed to be taken of them. If Caesar had
stabbed me, they would have done no less.

Victims of the Fall

This has been a good life. God does not send us a
cross any heavier than we can bear. How you cope is
the important thing, not the events themselves.

Your step-father has been so magnificent under a
tremendous strain which I don't think you appreciate
at all. He has been overly conscientious about you,
about me and about Philomena - in addition to his own
obligations. He has been so faithful in caring about us
all. It has really been unfair - the latest burden you
bring us. But then we are all part of God's grand
design, and we must accept personal tragedy in our
lives as part of the eternal mystery.

Love Mother

Bygones Begone

You have related what happened - you have admitted
that your conduct during marriage was indefensible
you pleaded guilty in the divorce proceedings. The
matter should be closed. The only unanswered
questions are those that are by their nature
unanswerable or by their implication unworthy of
consideration. My only regret is that I cannot put you
with all your armchair strategy, in the middle of the
A Shar valley and watch you stew as the enemy

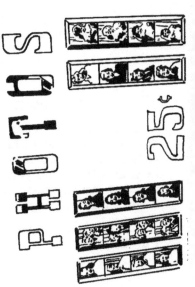

PHOTOS 25¢

artillery rounds are landing around your head.

The old man

Depends On How You Look At It

Congratulations! Your letter with enclosed photographs does a superb job of furthering the moral decay of this nation. The photo of two women (I gather one of them is your wife?) and yourself 'Relate in Near-by River' was just a little too much for my traditional values. When I was your age we 'related' with our clothes on.

If this is truly, as you say 'what's happening', then I'm dropping out.

Love Mother

On The Record

It's been a great '3' in every way. I love you.

Your No. 2 favourite

Different Kind of Affection

Explain Sodom and Reveal thyself. The Mysterium is babbling beyond comprehension.

Nightripper

Haunted Houses

I read with mounting horror your letter on this your second marriage. There can be no effective solution to the problem so long as you are in the corrupting grip of that Nightripper guy.

Love Mother

The Drugless Turn-On

I'm taking a soya bean powder drink and doing
exercises - have gained five pounds, still going.
Muscles in tone, more like a panther crouched to
spring rather than stuck pig. My new favourite
sensory stimuli: cashews to eat, roses to smell, fur
to feel and your photo to look at! Heck - baby like when
are we three going to really make it?

Your favourite Karate Kitten

Vision to Inspire

I suggest you join the local Humanist Social Group
(Air Conditioned) and take in Poisons in our Environment
- Can We Protect Ourselves? Loving oneself and
interacting with others. Trans-Sexualism-Life
Experience of a Male changing into a Female. And
maybe then this group will stick together after all.

Love your F.K.K.

P.S. Perhaps you can become an evangelist for
bisexuality?! Nightripper is all for the idea. He wants
to come up for the weekend - get here late tonight -
says he needs to get his tubes cleaned out. Well maybe
we can turn him on. Pick some yarrow to smoke, and
make tea with. What do you suggest? Anyway let's
space out baby - I'm finding the 3 routine pretty much
of a drag. And as for your Mom coming to stay with
us definitely NO - I know she's upset about your stepdad
leaving her but shit honey if she comes here then I'll
be splitting.

Feud in the Hills

If you want me to ever unlock this door and let you in
please obey the following rules:

1. Don't touch anything
2. Don't move anything
3. Don't take anything
4. Don't say anything
5. Wait until I've put on my robe, turned off the lights, have my first smoke and smile - then shoot.

Your snowbound unicorn

Echoes From An Unhappy Past

Today I received your very understanding letter. Thank you so much. May I revert 'very briefly' and lastly to the quite sad state of my sister's life. When thrown from her horse when about 19 years old she was an expert horsewoman and a very beautiful figure in the hunting field (a boy trespassing rode his bicycle behind horse my sister had loosened the reins hence the fall) breaking small bones in nose and while immediate Dr's care was given my sister did not, would not receive further care this through the years caused indeterminate brain tissue damage - the nervous system becoming uncontrollably worse. Your fine grandfather's sudden death he was an educated good man (bleeding to death in his home shocked sister). I returned at that cause only to go through a most terrifying experience. Your mother was kid 14 I believe, such a pretty girl but a very frightened child her responsibilities were greater than one can understand two very undisciplined sisters and unruly brothers all of which was the elder sister's care for no compensation, abuse mentally and physically. This I even related to by blood was petrified dreadful letters were sent to me and mine. Then I again visited only to encounter such to me unheard of mad behaviour. Your mother was homeless because of the 'way of life' which had become part of the 'system'. I then rented a house for we both were very happy. We had outside visitors bobbing up and down outside our abode and the names we were called were quite a revelation. We decided one eve to walk awhile only to encounter a dreadful experience. Your dad had been plied with drink and he came direct to me arm in arm with two women and punched me in my mouth damaging my lips and teeth. I had to resort to court action. These and other unbelievable activities did hasten my return to my home (WC). Your mother visited me later and was very lovely and well behaved as I had always found her to be. I understood quite well what anyone in your mother's position had and would contend with. Your mother as I analyze it has been abominably treated. Her poor pre-age mother at 40 needed long past time attention and how your mother did live through all this abuse I know not. I do feel however that in her love for you, in her best to give protective efforts she should be given the utmost care that is positively possible. She is a good soul and there will be great comfort for you to know that if your good mother can come home to us we in turn will provide and share that which we have which would also extend to survivor's half of estate in other words we would proceed to adopt and care for her to our demise and half survivor's estate to wit. I hope you can read this and forgive its longevity but I would like you and your dear wife to get to know me not without faults, not senseless but knowing each to his own and love begets love, friends through the years, pride in self, analysis of other people's God given right to live their own lives as long as we are not asked to join in their disharmony then we live and let live. Please write and love to you both.

Aunt Margene

The Irish Troubles

You ask about your great-grandfather he was a small
Irish farmer (three inches taller than his father's
father) and thought about sex all the time. He thought
about it with the kine in the byre, with the peat in the
bog and with the kelp on the strand and sometimes at
night he would rouse himself on his pallet with dreadful
groans, exclaiming 'Oh, I am thinking about sex again',
this was so painful to the rest of the family, who slept
like spoons in the big bed beside and slightly above his
pallet, that they arranged for him to be shipped to the
colonies. His favourite benediction was 'May the wind
be always at your back, may the roads rise up to meet
you, may you live to be 101, and when you do come to
die may you be in Heaven 6 months before the devil
knows you've gone.' And so I repeat this for you and
your dear wife (in the photo you sent me I was not
sure which of the two extremely pretty ladies either
side of you is your wife?) and please know that if
there is anything else of the family history you wish
to know I shall only be too happy to oblige.

Love Aunt Margene

One More Time

How come you never write to me? Did I mention in
my last letter that I've bought a lovely leopard
turtleneck playsuit in acetate jersey (to bring out the
tiger in you?!) and it has a zipper front so I can wear
it open or closed. Oh honey please come back, darling
pet monkey I'm not human without your warm eyes.
I didn't know how much I was going to love - I was a
kid when we were married, even if I was twenty-two.
Now I'm a woman. You made me one. And a woman
wants her man with her.

Love your wife always

100

Stereophonic Superman

You're so concerned with all that motivational soul-
searching. One of the requirements to get where I'm
at is that you have to dig fucking and doping. If you've
got that going then you're human, at least, and maybe
you can learn to do something useful. It's impossible
to know what the effect of living with me will be. I
think it'll be like a time bomb - that the effect will
become known later. All of a sudden you'll see how
influential it is. But it'll have to ferment until it pops
out in your consciousness. I like the new. I want you
to have a toothpick in your ear and a purple boot on
your right foot. But there you are in a gold metal joy
suit, zapped into a wall socket and sexlessly a/ceeing
and d/ceeing your artificial heart. Maybe after all
you need a certain type of mentality such as might be
found in a menopausal Roman Catholic lesbian. But if
your mind is orientated towards fantasy instead of
life then of coursé you should forget the whole thing.
Anyway the purpose of this letter is to save the anal-
compulsive researcher in you some trouble by putting
down stuff you haven't perhaps heard before, and also
to offer more-or-less concrete (instead of neo-
religious) information to you who ought to know where
you stand in the Cosmic order of Things.

Your Karate Kitten

Home Sweet Zoo

I haven't heard from you for so long, maybe your
wife has eaten you? Will you be home for Christmas?
You know I'm on my own now, and I have no intention
of going over to Margene's place, and as for staying on
here well I am o.k. but get lonesome often. What
would I ever do without you? As for money well your
poor father used to say 'I throws all the money up in

the air and what stays up is the Lord's what comes down is mine. ' Did I ever tell you that because he loved animals so, I put a watering trough in front of his grave. A sheep lambed on his grave and I think he would have liked that. When I visit his grave now I weep to think how I could have married again well I think that monster is living out a most terrible fate brought about by his own actions, and must now be suffering an ugly species of character assassination. However much he has fallen in my eyes, and others, it is probably in the deeper recesses of his own mind that he is suffering most and experiencing the harshest judgements.

Well I must close now. Do come over for Christmas you know this town ain't all a good place and it ain't all a bad place and your presence would make it better. Please don't tell me to go over to Margene's 'cos she's an arthritically gnarled stick of a woman who wets her bed is only intermittently coherent and has to be spoon-fed by her other sister, who tends her with a tactful if exasperated saintliness, and her husband is either dotty or drunk, and they are all hypochondriacs at that pig farm, give them a lovable set of old bones such as mine and bingo, bango, they'll supply a fatal disease and buy the funeral. Please write soon.

Love Mother

When It Is Over

In your recent note you claim to be a well-hung stud, 11 inches and thick - I mean that's a little hard to take. And it's probably not true, either. I mean it's like saying I'm a gospel-spouting nymphomaniac, performing in several stages of undress once on the floor and once on a bed. As far as I'm concerned your love life is your own business from now on I just want out. My attitude towards love has changed a lot as a result of our brief, ill-fated menage.

K.K.

Romantic Backlash

You wanted our relationship to be successful, I wanted it to be outrageous. We had the power to make things happen and the whole idea was to do that, and now you are a shadow of your former lustrous mystical self. It's a farce a big goof. I think it was necessary for us to first love and then hate you, and now we must learn to understand you. You had a dream of something beautiful, but your soul had a broken slave at its centre telling you the dream was a lie and that we were certain to fail. The dream was true but the slave chained the three of us. Now we are free and the dream will be honoured with flesh. You were a corrupt prophet but we have at last come out of the wilderness.

Your Karate lover

Painful Re-Entry

C'mon and get it motherfucker!

Love your future

Soldier-Cowpoke

Good luck, brother & love. Our blood will be mingling in the streets before this game is over. But let us remember who the enemies are and not waste our energy fighting each other.

Nightripper

Somewhat Deflating

What you say about what you're doing is your rap. But what counts is what you're doing. Whether you're living the life or not. If you're not, the rest is beside the point.

Love K.K.

Slightly Surrealistic

Art should not be merely a luxury for the rich but available to everyone. So I'm sending you a Planetary Folklore participation kit. You'll find all the pieces are snugly interlocking circles and squares, and there's a small suction cup provided for easy manipulation. The Kit also includes programmed directions - each piece is coded on the back - but it's best to figure out your own scheme, and that way you may learn something about taste and design.

Happy Xmas.

Love Dad

P.S. Did I tell you I have had special bracing put inside my car door and it has a good reassuring thunk when I close it - the kind of sound you get when you drop a rice pumpkin in the mud - a kind of clump - not a clink, clatter or clunk, but a CLUMP. It's real good.

Ambition's Reward

All I wanted in life once was for you to grow up to be a decent citizen. I was happy with our family on the whole and all I needed was to wake up in the morning and hear the birds. That gave me joy. I used to go to church, as you know, and the preacher would talk about

God, Jesus and the Bible. Now he tells me why I
shouldn't buy grapes. Life is getting faster and furiouser
and there's a lack of friendliness. No closeness. Half
the time I don't even know who my neighbour is, unless
there's a fight. Sometimes I feel like throwing up my
hands and going so far back in the hills they'll have to
pipe sunshine in. Still I've only got a few more years
to contend with it all.

You know you have still a few belongings here - where
shall I send them? To wit: 1 tube of spot remover, 1
small tin of shoe polish, 1 pair of sunglasses, 6 packets
of matches, 1 toothbrush (without toothpaste), 3 pencils
(2 broken) and for some reason, best known to yourself
I guess: 350 ballpoint pens. 1 loafer tassel, 3 unpaid
bills, 1 cheque book, 2 note pads, 1 Chop stick, 1 safety
pin, 6 paper clips, 9 rubber bands, 1 bottle of eye
drops, 1 pen light, 1 railroad timetable, 1 road map,
and some letters.

Love Mother

P.S. Although I'm not, as you know, a Mormon, I
really have come to believe that 'men will be punished
for their own sins and not for Adam's transgressions'.

Baffling Phenomenon

Seen at some distance you loom like a tower of onyx
robed in slashed summer clouds. Peer closer and
you become a full-lipped flower bitten by the sun,
bleeding pollen. I think I'm going to have an operation
that will blot out my memory.

Your X-wife

Illuminating Restraint

As far as the latest activities you seem to be committed

105

to are concerned we expected it. However, under no circumstances, will I be affected whatever by them. But let me say I'm upset about your absolute disregard for law and order and any kind of convention. It isn't the clothes. Hell, when I was a kid, I wore bell-bottom pants to school with silver bells on the side. But when I was your age, I couldn't wait to get out and get a piece of capitalism and become part of the Establishment. To you the future is obviously nothing. To me it is everything. It's sad. It's very sad. You want it all right now, the things it took me a lifetime to get. You don't know what work is when I was your age I'd sweat so much salt that when I undressed my pants stood up by themselves. Sometimes you have the air of a panhandler who tries to charm one into letting go two bits and only succeeds in embarrassing one. Your decisions suffer from a poverty of ideas. I am not offering a raft of new ideas either. I stand on the goals I have already set. I acknowledge that we still have vast problems that cannot be solved with our own resources. But at least I admit my mistakes and have learned from them. Man was made out of the soft earth and woman was made of a hard rib. Work is the answer to an awful lot of problems, just plain hard work.

The old man

Tastes Differ

What kind of a place do you want then - a cave of winds redecorated as a 19th century gentleman's club, retaining lacquered snuffboxes?

Your honeydove

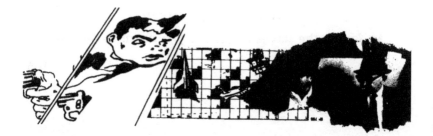

Mischiavellian Maneuver

Please call us. Not mad just want to talk. Love you and concerned.

Mother

Matter of Conscience

You ask how I am - well you could say I've been going to hell with myself but at least I'll hang on to my immortal soul.

Your X-wife

On Further Analysis

There seems now to be a slowly emerging conviction that the effects of our decisions are beginning to become visible. Look this is like the old debate about the glass of water. Is it half full or half empty? Do we put the emphasis on the aspect that the measures haven't worked as fast or as strongly as we had hoped, or on the aspect that they are in fact, working? An occasional doze of overcaution and lack of imagination may not always be a bad thing, that sometimes the best thing to do is nothing. But how much is your life governed by feelings? The trick is to make the emotion work for you, instead of against you. You need frank feed back on who you are, when you get that you become so much more honest that you're bound to function better. If you really insist on a divorce only after a year I feel that such a move would inevitably lead to perpetuating and continuing the confusion between us all. I think this is a defeatist attitude - defeatist in terms of what it would accomplish. I do not think it's in the interest of our family. Have you really considered all the possible consequences?

The old man

Call It Hate

Towards the end of our marriage I really did find that
it had all turned into ugly realities and violent fantasies,
and instead of illuminating them, you simply lay down
and rolled around in them. Frankly I'm stunned. Never
in my wildest nightmare did I believe this could happen
to me. You seem only happy when you shock me,
delirious when you infuriate me, but it seems you have
no defence when you bore me. So let's get rid of this
arid, devastated plethora of nothingness before I die of
boredom. You are so often like the kid walking up an
escalator that's going down, and it seems to me that
you dream incessantly of some dramatic Lourdes where
the healing miracle of instant greatness will occur,
and you live in a fantasy world like Disneyland - a tidy
mini-world which works on paper just like it is supposed
to but once you start living in the real world you make
it seem like a befouled, tense and faltering civilization.
Once upon a time, when a child, we were taught about
the three genders: masculine, feminine and neuter.
At long last, I understand the purpose of the neuter.
When we first met you were jaunty impudent, stylish,
full of a cocky wit, an irresistible energy, a balanced
awareness of your own burgeoning health and the wetness
behind your ears. Now you somehow manage to be both
fawning and snotty at the same time. Instead of energy
you have an irritating and clumsy effrontery, a puerile
brashness, a sweaty freneticism. You grow on me like
cancer. You would never have treated me the way you
did if you thought anything of me. Maybe some women
would fall for that line but not me. I've been lucky, my
mother clued me in. I know the score.

Some day you might meet a girl who wants to take a
correspondence course. You use letters like scatter-
shit. Please don't bother answering this letter I don't
want any more mountains of waffle papers. Optimism
is a scarce and somewhat foolhardy commodity these

days, but I'll risk it and bet on a quieter life this fall.

Your X-wife

Was That Trip Necessary?

You might like to know that the old man had a heart attack at 12.10 June 15th, sitting in a green chair - whoever pulls the cards out of the rack upstairs, wasn't ready to pull his.

Rescue Ahead?

I don't know what you did to poor Bu-Bu, but he had a breakdown soon after you left, and what with tending to my daughter and her hives and hysteria, and then the old man having a heart attack, all in the same day I really felt I wasn't going to be able to make it. Anyway things are a little clearer now, and I have the time to write you at long last.

I found the most beautiful place for Bu-Bu to have a rest cure, a real treat to go there. Each room is designed in an aesthetic colour scheme (are dogs really colour blind?) with appointments to match, including a full floor carpet and separate cathedral, sky-lighted ceiling. The attendants are something to see, dressed in Spanish gold uniforms embellished with a crest that boasts 'Singulare Ministerium' (Singular Service?). There are promises of demand feeding, attention to each guest's quirks, soothing music and active social programme. The grooming service rivals my own beauty parlour. There's the choice of a 5-foot-by-4-foot 'efficiency apartment' or a 13-foot-by-6-foot family suite. Each room has a 25-foot-long backyard, an intercom so that the dog can be soothed by a disembodied voice, a 3-inch-thick mattress colour-coordinated to a

wall-to-wall carpet, and raised feeding bowls so that
a dog doesn't have to stoop for his supper, and a constant
supply of smells. I almost wanted to stay there myself
instead of returning here to witness my daughter's
ravings, a raging cataclysmic mad scene. I couldn't
help feeling that her every action was motivated. Even
her words were transformed into an eloquent cascade
of accusation, bitter mockery, and finally deranged
wailing. And there was the old man acting as if nothing
was out of the usual daily routine (I guess he's gotten
used to our daughter's mad scenes) anyway we had
guests for dinner and he rose from the table and began
to tell us of the virtues of squid with mayonnaise 'it
exerts a favourable influence on metabolism' he said
'and is prescribed for persons with heart problems.'
Well I guess that was kind of o.k. but later, very
drunk, he suddenly shouted out 'what I must have is a
helicopter shot of our garden covered with nothing but
naked women - all the way to the horizon.' Our guests
(one unhappily an effete jet-setter and the other one of
the Beautiful People) thought this very funny. Secretly
I feel I'm living in Bellevue, and in a way, I guess, I
don't blame you for finally getting out, and I realize
that you are now being cautious as a singed cat due to
the traumatic experiences through which you have passed.
Do you still tap your prominent teeth with your right
index finger - I always took that as the danger signal of
boredom and displeasure.

I don't want to go into the past too much, but I often
think of a certain night spent with you in my car. Do
you know ever since that time there's been an impressive
'budda-deh-buddedeh' in my rear axle, and a scintillating
'chatcheteh-chatch-eteh' comes from a rear shock
absorber. There's a soothing 'toketah, toketah' from
my radio antenna, and a 'tosshhhzbbd' from my radio!

I've joined an encounter-therapy group and am being
converted to the 'new ethic', but do you know after ten

minutes of sharing an experience in the encounter group
I was back to being hurt by people. Limitations of the
experience became evident. I could carelessly caress
any member of my five-person group but I still said
'excuse me' if my leg brushed another's from a different
group. And some guy next to me suddenly blurted out
'this entire scene brings to mind the sex life of the
praying mantis if the male mantis makes an error in
his sexual approach, the female bites off his head.'
Then just as I was leaving someone came up to me and
said 'if you're good if you're healthy, you'll scream
loud, you'll emote, you'll love, if you can't, you're
sick.' These words stuck with me, and I feel more and
more that I cannot possibly flourish (or even survive)
in this climate of mindless emotionalism and restrictive
fear-driven rigidity. I want to leave. Will you let me
know by return where we can meet, or call me by collect.
You know before you left I felt I had an almost telepathic
ability to anticipate your needs. I feel right at this
moment you need me. I've always believed that you have
great courage, that you can be loyal, and do tell the
truth, insofar as you can, and that your destiny is not
to be evil, and that you need a woman who can mobilize
and release the good qualities that you have in you. I
recognized your melancholy sense of the doomed,
repetitive quality of our family life pattern, and that
you were invaded and disturbed by a sense of the lost
ifs that determined our lives. Not to sound foolish but
I feel we are meant for each other.

Madame Moustache!

P.S. Put your trust in God, she will provide!

Continuing Struggle

I am sending along with some of your belongings a
little momento that belonged to your poor father, a

cigarette lighter in the form of a cross. Take good care of it, as he did. I'm not sure if it still works, and if it doesn't you can get it seen to.

I had a real surprise the other day, your wife's mother suddenly called me up, wanted to know where you were, of course I didn't tell her. Anyway she came round, seemed very upset, her face smeared with blotches of cosmetics as if to ward off the angel of death. No doubt each Friday or Saturday she allows a Mr. Henri to resurrect her hair from its New York Post grey to a colour that resembles a mustard-stained counter, which she must think is blonde. She obviously refuses to admit her ballroom days are over. She talked a lot about you, but it was as if she spoke of someone else, certainly not my son I kept thinking. She apparently sees you in part a victim of your own promises and record, and strangely enough a kind of tightly wound man with a gaunt face and the physique of a working bantamweight! And for some reason she presumed I was ashamed of my heritage, and that this was also a hangup with yourself. She said things like: 'You don't have to spend most of your time explaining to people that where you come from doesn't have anything to do with who you personally are. I come from dirt-farming country, my daddy was a dirt farmer, and I'm proud of that.' She really seemed slightly cranky to me, and talked on and on about this dirty farmer father of hers, who apparently escorted her to her room each night where they would give each other 'rub-downs'. And her departing words were something about getting a shotgun because she wants to be ready when the 'shit starts coming down'. I watched her get into her chauffeur driven car and could swear she was wearing a hip enhancer, you know (or maybe you don't?) one of those terrible hidden foam rubber pads that are supposed to give your hipline outline a rounded curve. She shouted from the car, and you know how deaf I am in my left ear, but anyway I think the words were 'the only true hero is a dead hero'. I'm sure glad I didn't let her know where you are for I have a feeling that she's out for some terrible kind of revenge. Well take care of yourself and write me soon.

Love Mother

Another Death Plot?

You came to our place looking for something; I found something - maybe myself. Please call.

'Mammy Pleasant'

Matter of Prediction

You impressed me with your effort to be serious, but the time spent with you has taken a heavy toll. A gruesome botch. A pretentious pitifully empty fraud. I gave you the benefit of the doubt originally and feel embarrassed to think of my words of praise. What struck then was your resonance, but now it sounds to me totally hollow. Now I feel that I was naive to be taken in by your practically non-stop claims to significance. The emperor is stark naked. You are a pompous bore, and I am frequently all but sickened by the void beneath your solemn agonies, you're not cruel but nasty, not clever but self-conscious, not obscure but merely vague. And our relationship was like a conventional melodrama, formal, contrived, milking me like a cow, squeezing every ounce of bitter-sweet irony from our closed-in life. And now since I'm writing about all that and I am already pretty angry, I may as well get out of my system all my angry stuff.

You, there, a rotten, no good stinking, cowardly snickering, stupid squirming yellow bastard with your

stupid creaking ugly voice I am still so disgusted with
you that I don't ever want to hear your answer. I have
only this to tell you: WATCH OUT! Remember this:
watch out, on your way home. I'll be there, in the dark
street, waiting for you with a heavy hot splicer in my
hand, and you should begin to count your seconds by
the time you finish reading this letter. I'm not going
to reveal what I'm going to do to you, you horrible
creature, destroyer of everything I hold to as beautiful,
watch out, this is my first warning!

Your X

P.S. You are an ideological eunuch whose most
comfortable position is straddling the ideological fence.
You are a parasite of passion, a merchant of hate, and
a vulture. We can afford to separate people like you
from our society with no more regret than we should
feel over discarding rotten apples from a barrel.

Pullout

I didn't find your letter all that inspiring - pleasant
enough but the energy level was almost zero. First you
see me, then you don't. Somehow not very much of it
amused me, and (to summarize) have decided to live
a more private life. It's good for one's mythology. I
appear at parties in numerous disguises and hardly
ever introduce myself. This cuts down on the bullshit.

Love K.K.

Diverting Talent

I've got the chauvinistic shakes. I can't fight your ideas,
or sink into them, because from my vantage point it
would be more effective if all that power would produce
some thorns before flowers. Why is it that you always

astoundingly manifest the light side of a Shakespearian clown who has read Reich? And frankly your sense of an orgy is a bourgeois fun machine, an ensemble madness amidst velour curtains and chaises longues. It has the predicaments of farce (the secret rendezvous, the hidden lover, the fool-proof plan) and your laughter affirms a world of jaded wealth, sweaty affaires, passions conceived out of boredom, and a fascination with gadgets and games of the nouveaux riches. As for your erotic fantasies well they're the kind that make horny, middle-aged businessmen sibilate the litany 'this is shit - what is this shit?' And your ideas have the idiot simplicity of a high school sorority hazing. Sometimes I feel you are afflicted with some virulent form of foot and mouth disease. And I can't even recommend you to my analyst, he's a schitzy shrink with hidden camera and two-way mirrors, and somehow he always gets me into the state of a white-faced nympho sucking my polyploid fingers as I writhe on a tabletop, and his favourite slogan for almost any trauma is 'don't panic'.

As for youknowwho well I'm all for us three to live together, at least she would be a presence not lacking subjective depth who is interestingly problematic. Vis-a-vis dangerous emotions connected with sex. At the moment she seems to be the canary who swallowed the cat - an impressive, if somewhat unnatural act. She has somehow gotten hold of two feathered freaks: scarlet parrots that can hang on, I guess, until a hundred. They sit complacently on either shoulder, kiss you and lick your tongue (optional) and sometimes I squeeze a little grape juice on her nipples where they suck.

Love K.K.

Rattling the Cage

If reconciliation is not our goal, why are we still
fighting? It takes time to work these things out but each
time we talk to each other my frustration escalates.
Your last outrageous charges and innuendoes have
represented the most vicious assassination effort. You
endanger our relationship and its growth by defining its
limits, forgetting that every relationship defines its own
limits, because part of its motivational thrust is the
need to discover its intended direction, perhaps to
attempt to get beyond what its nature won't allow it get
beyond.

In short Aquarian guerrilla you sound as revolutionary
as one of the Knights of Columbus.

Madame Moustache

Herculean Change

Any attempt to pump life and humour into such a corpse
as you have become is like fucking a mattress.

K.K.

No New Skeletons

I can well understand why you left your first wife, she
is crazy and that goes for the rest of that family. I have
just returned from their place, after suddenly being
cabled to go there. I thought perhaps you had returned,
but no, it turned out they wanted to find out where you
were, the reasons I guess best known to yourself?

Anyway when I arrived there I was met by your ex-wife,
meanwhile riding the range in a black Lincoln
Continental, and a white Continental respectively both
Mr. and Mrs. drove like armored tanks over the open

pastureland. When Mr. got out his daughter treated him to a cadet response, clicking her heels, throwing back her shoulders and saying 'yes sir' in a loud voice. Mr. ushered me into his office, huge fireplace, gilded mirror, eagles on door-knobs, the works (you never really talked about their place?). Anyway the old man, face pink, healthy-looking hands carefully manicured, with gold at his wrists and silk at his throat and wrinkles on his neck, and looking as though he'd been dieting, kept lighting cigars with a disposable lighter with a removable gold case. 'My days are simple, ' he said and then went on (he spoke as though he'd memorized a script two lines at a time) about your marriage and the breakup. He talked about it all as though his daughter had ordered ice cream rather than apple pie, mentioned that she was unhappy, about you leaving, for a day, but she got over it. 'Parental-type power must be exercised. ' And then for some reason he began talking about his chauffeur who I gathered had suddenly left that morning, taking one of their cars, and some money. 'The niggers have got it made they keep closing in and closing in, working their way into everything. They're even playing cowboys. If a bunch of good ol' briashopper Ku Kluxers had got ahold of Martin Luther King he wouldn't have lived as long as he did. ' I was naturally shaken by this time, mentioned God, and do you know what he then said? (This actually was later at dinner during which he gave a running commentary on each course giving its origin - sometimes down to the name of the cow they slaughtered for the beef.) Well he bellowed out: 'I don't frankly care whether God is dead, blind or just out to lunch. ' He stared with mock malevolence at me across his tossed salad, and slowly raised a pointed finger from an imaginary holster, and cried 'Zap! Whammo! Jesus I've still got it. ' He was, of course, by that time completely pissed, and his wife was trying to ignore the fact, dressed in a peekaboo linear jumpsuit, ironically enough trying to

come on strong as the consummately sensible and strong
female, sharp-tongued and absolutely clear-eyed, and
while he with eyes raised in mock piety, squinted in
suspicion, went on shouting things like 'I have no
regrets. I do not intend to repudiate my beliefs, recant
my words, or run and hide.' She whispered 'don't take
too much notice of his off-the-cuff blunders. These days
his atrocities are premeditated. He seems unable to
help it.' Then your ex-wife chipped in and said something about 'daddy, you know, keeps in his desk a list
of men, killers all, who were spared the gas chamber
and went on to murder another 22 people.' And the whole
time he went on shouting out stories about his life in the
early days, punctuated with bammos and whistles, arm
waving and mimicry, he might well have been regaling
a bunch of boys around a campfire. I must admit out of
the three of them your mother-in-law struck me as
the most sane, but somewhat dotty, and taken up with
herself. I unfortunately commented on her jumpsuit
and she went into a long account of the store she'd got
it finally rounding up with 'isn't it divine of course it's
the uniform of the '70s and as you can see it fits so
tightly that getting into it is a chore.' All this followed
by showing me some photos of herself in low-cut gown,
shot from above, and in jumpsuit, shot from below.
Meanwhile Mr. was back onto his chauffeur 'one has
to consider the evidence that the Negro may be inherently
inferior to the white and incapable of competing with
him - look at the ones who have succeeded they're
almost all light-coloured.'

Finally the crunch came, was I intending to marry
you! What do they want of you? Do you owe the old
man money? Is the menopausal jumpsuit bitch lusting
after you? Is she out for revenge? I just don't know,
but all the time I had the impression they were trying
to warn me not to shack up with you. Well as you know
since K.K. left I'm all for it, marriage included!

Can't you just see us hitting that middle road: you'll
wear white starched shirts, suits with baggy pants,
white ankle-high cotton socks. Toothpicks. Lunch in
a paper sack. Off-duty bourbon and 7-up. And I'll wear
a wire stiff bouffant, girdle, at-the-knee print dresses
and save Green stamps, and be active in the Girl Scouts
and PTA. A Bible adorns the coffee table, and there'll
be a flag decal on the family car. I'll live for 'the kids'.
And we'll survive in a gritty decayed inner-city
neighbourhood. A treat will be dinner at the Burger
King. And family fun will be a Sunday drive, a backyard
hamburger barbecue, or watching T.V. Darling I can't
wait - can you?

Love your snowey unicorn

Unanswered Mail

Please let me know how you are - interested and
bothered. Anxious.

Love Mother

I turned on the bed that creaked only to my own
creakings. And theirs? My oral-erotic X-wife I no
longer heard. Asleep? A mask to slip over your eyes
to induce profounder sleep, ear-plugs to ditto. Maybe
this was one of those States that had a number of
antiquated sex laws, I could accuse him of 'lascivious
carriage' i. e. conduct which is wanton, lewd or lustful
and tending to produce voluptuous emotions. All that

was needed to prove 'lascivious carriage' was some sign of sexual activity. Outside I moved along the walls. Their door. An infamous gunslinger. Up the side of the mighty fissure speeds the colourfully costumed figure. Be yer age ya know it ain't loaded you checked it only this morning. But the gun gave proof to my hand, hooded thoughts. A mystery man was terrifying the town's women - was he just a crank, or a dangerous sex fiend?

And as our soliloquizing stalwart makes the key-hole scene I thought well why not. The easy way can help delay early climax, prolong pleasure, satisfy X-wife, she'll then thrill with sensations I evoke in her. Just before we divorced she was fairly wised up on interpreting the interrelationships of mutual fulfilment. Between organisms and my alpine tundra environment. Horse hair inner-sewen between cushiony layers. The perfectly balanced matching boxspring. This with individually wire-tied spring steel coils. Ridiculously big brakes; they take the panic out of panic stops. Needle-sharp steering; you can flick your way around trouble. And anatomically shaped seats that keep you seated. Principle industry: contemplation of the past. The result a sharpened alchemy of perception and sensation.

Through the keyhole I saw an extraordinary globe-girdling exercise in private diplomacy. She was wearing that damned mind-blast orange highbuttoned dress, unbuttoned to the navel, and looked like a colossus painted in bright harlot colours. A billboard deity. Her face, breasts, buttocks, femurs, forearms arbitrarily interchanged. A product of a daffy plastic surgeon who forgot how to put the jigsaw puzzle together. But flickering clearly in that chaos of flesh was a small smile of mockery, resentment and desire. I closed my eyes for a brief moment and saw earlier figures that were everywhere and nowhere, neither inside nor outside, living in a perplexing world of spatial ambiguity. Looking again I saw his shadow above the bed, a dragonfly roof supported by Y-trusses which had the soar of enormous seabirds. He was, I must admit, a brilliant surprise. Almost legendary for his flamboyant dramatic effects, all fidelity and restraint in a performance that minimized Teutonic heroics. Propelled by rhythms that even when slow never faltered. Very soon my chest tightened. Almost simultaneously I experienced a loosening of the urinary tract that spelled excitement. I aimed at their door, and thought this is a scene where selling yourself enjoys a downright metaphysical sanction. The dilemma of the sensitive intellectual caught in the nowhere land between progressive ideals and primitive practices. But why short-circuit yourself? Can you tell when your thinking blocks your feelings and feelings block thinking?

I stumbled into my room. Exhausted and dejected. The psyche has been hurt, and the pain of loss is sharpened by the thought of what might have been. The past reared again. A rotating globe with raised topographic features, a large lunar hemisphere which changes phases, and swells into a series of winding terraces. A spiral staircase without visible support falls on frozen seas. The thrust of a rocket furrowing white sand. It grows as it goes. A hotbed of unrest. Here and behind me in the next room. If I made a hole in the wall perhaps it would permit an inspection of dinosaur bones in their original positions, allowing themselves to be uncovered in high relief rather than removed. This idea provided a worthwhile orientation. But soon layers of the formation clearly exposed by the fault took over. I well knew she was sneaky. Diabolic in her cunning. So innocent that her deliberate naivete became a defence, a premonitory mea culpa. Why the hell didn't I split right away. Leave them to it. Crack down on the

madness and unhealthy situation which was rapidly
enveloping. A difference between responsible dissent
and storm-trooper bullying or throwing myself down in
the road, smashing windows and rowdyism. Why not
admit women were misanthropic totems, man-eaters
at once seductive and savage. I could take him aside.
Prove that I was a master of the broken line and the
ingratiating curve. That nothing is rigid and antiseptic.
Appear clean-cut, uncomprising, agree where we can
and try to limit and restrict the impact of differences.
Thoroughly effective. They lunge at each other but no
longer in hate and rage, instead they laugh, their
eyes sparkling with friendship. And I'd watch his
diminutive figure retreat in the night. Beautiful.
Wouldn't have missed it for anything.

But how does he see me?
Steel-rimmed glasses
sideburns
semi-successful moustache
a wool cap pulled far forward
striding along the sidewalks
leaning into the wind
fists jammed into pockets
shoulders hunched

| Intense | idealistic | impatient | gentle |
| radical | intellectual | direct | shrewd |

No. Possibly old and impotent, with a future as narrow
as my shoulders, striding along like some sort of sage-
brush propelled by winds of unknown origin. Having a
penchant for delay, gross, clear, conspicuous,
transparent conflict of interest. A child whose nose
ran all winter, who missed anywhere from 25% to 30%
of a school year, flinched when a teacher dared so much
as to reach out an arm and sat painfully aware that to
the other students in the elementary school he was just
another member of the family 'out there on the side of
that hill without enough to eat'.

And from what she has told him of our marriage? A pictorial exhibit of cannibal life. A dropout of the pioneer mother. Exorcising doppelgangers of every-day psychoses by giving her parents for Christmas 3 fancy cans of elephant meat from Kenya. And what a Christmas that was! She had the night before turned herself on in a new dress. An undulation of gossamer-fine Italian polyester knit. Floating, draping, defining the figure in the most subtle terms. Trumpet shaped sleeves, the kind Chinese emperors tucked tiny pets into. She refused to let me get anywhere near her as she stepped around the room, on the bed, in front of the mirror, in her gleaming patent leather. Starting a chain reaction with double doses of gold-toned hardware on the buckled vamp. Rhinestone studded heels that played music every time she took a step. It was a robust climax to a week of low-keyed progress reports. I thought of hypnotizing her, but she had hypnotized herself. I left, got pissed, returned and tore up some rose bushes.

The following morning inevitably I was summoned by her father to the briefing room. Usually he looked like he was fresh from a taxidermist's shop. That morning he doffed his glasses, discarded his syntax, and launched into a stem-winding 37-minute sermon. His ad lib speech drew liberally on generalities and platitudes, and even a garbled quote from the Bible. He explained solemnly: 'I think that if you saw a little child in this room who was trying to waddle across the floor and some big bully came along and grabbed it by the hair and started stomping it I think you'd do some-thing about it.' He pounded his palms together for emphasis, dry-washed his hands, milked his fingers and sawed the air with extravagant gestures. Throughout the session he modulated his mood between exasperation, patience and mellowness. Though he here seems to be unhappy to all appearances – and in this case had good reason to be so - some who have worked with him say that his turned-down-mouth expression is really one of concentration on the matter before him. When he is really displeased, they say, his most characteristic expression is a tight smile, accompanied by excessive politeness. Finally, as if exhausted by the whole situation, he took out his pocketknife salted and sliced an apple: 'I've always been an apple man - they're good and they don't have many calories and I've always eaten apples - have one.'

As it turned out it was the day of his 33rd anniversary, later at dinner he presented an Italian tapestry to his wife with a kiss and a comment that 'it's the prettiest thing I ever saw'. His wife gave him a pig. 'She's moody. Some mornings she'll have nothing to do with me. She can be very mean. She sometimes bites. Her diet consists of corn and a pig mash and she doesn't care for garbage. She's a great point of dissension between my wife and me. My wife has Bu-Bu and he's scared to death of pigs - but you can house-train pigs, you know. I would like to be able to have her in our living room.'

He was all for reconciliations, and while slicing through a neatly tiered 3-layer cake - more like a marble cake full of unexpected whorls and inseparable blendings - he exclaimed 'I do not think that those men who are out there fighting for us tonight think we should enjoy the luxury of fighting each other back home.' After dinner it was time for one of those famous family outings. Time for the year's reckoning, and this investor was far from pleased with the results. By every major measure of the situation the past 6 months had been nothing but a garland of losses. If other investors couldn't find comfort in this common misery, at least they knew that the drab first half was over. Finally the widely expected new programme got under way. I left without saying a word. Always on the defensive, and you get sucked into the golden sluice anyway.

I went to a burlesque show and watched an unutterable
tacky gaggle of bathos-laden drag queens at an
impoverished homemade ball. For ten minutes a coy
bit of fellow fondled his flaccid cock with sexless ennui.
From this Roman circus I found myself somewhere
amidst silverware that jangled along with sensuous
whispering of plastic trays sliding over steel railings.
My cheeseburger spat contemptuously at the matron
who flipped it. The meat was quickly silenced by the
bun that drank its red juice all the way past the cash
register and into the dining room, where I sat
inconspicuously in front of a huge picture window that
looked out on a scene gone mad with the first jab of
frigidity - a frigidity that would paralyze unadorned
flesh until May. There is a message in all this madness,
I thought. Homosexuality, heterosexuality and
asexuality all merge into one broad spoof of religious
sentiment. The main thing, they say, is to know
yourself so that nothing human will ever be alien to
you. An unprecedented freedom, but a freedom only
to switch channels: AC/DC. Anyway what's it to us in
the time of Apollo? Two of our kind stand with their own
four feet on the moon. Two earthlings representing both
sexes (though they are men) all races (though they are
pinkish-white beneath their white space suits) and all
nations (though they are from the United States, as you
might infer from the patches on their sleeves). How far,
after all, is the moon from earth? Precisely the same
distance as Vietnam - across the living room. 'The
moon is our backyard' says one influential member of
the White House task group. 'This is no longer pie-
in-the-sky a few pioneers may even decide to live
there - inside plastic bubbles, dining on algae cultures
and recycling their fluid wastes.' As for noxious waste
disposal, instead of dumping acids, poison gases,
pharmaceutical and petrochemical by-products and

X-wives into some convenient waterway, the new
alternative would be to drop them down craters.

On the way back, knowing my in-laws would be glazed-
eyed in front of T.V. belly-full of turkey and cranberry,
and petting their new acquisition: the pig. I made my
plan: rape. That's what was necessary. And it worked!
That night, well about 5 a.m. she succumbed. We rose
up slowly as if we didn't belong to the outside world
any longer like swimmers in a shadowy dream who
didn't need to dream. However a day later I was back
into my dreams. One night of rape was enough for me.
The shifting sands and whirlwinds, dust, cactus and
prairie dog howling were destined never to be re-enacted.
I really hadn't the stamina. To reach her meant a hard-
dug well with a stone casing built at ground level, while
I lowered myself by means of jackscrews, inch by inch.
One day I promised myself that I'd build a unique
memorial to perpetuate the memory of all my women.
Under a marble canopy would be life-size statues
showing us at various stages of our lives. A placard
embossed in gold with the words Erected mostly by
Hard labour. And as the executives peer down from
the twelfth-floor dining room, suspended in mid-air
by two steel girders, they would enjoy an unsurpassed
view of the carefully patterned banks of fern and
rhododendron which have been planted next to the
towering magnolia, the stand of eucalyptus surrounding
the canopy. A glass mosaic frames the entrance. Their
graves in the Chinese Garden surrounded by instant
antique Buddha heads, the corrosion of centuries having
been achieved by burying the newly minted statues in
urine-soaked ground for 3 months. My third wife would
love that, she had a shortcut way to a kind of Zen living.
Her inconsistency a kind of grace, tamed to a large
extent by levees, dams and spillways she discovered by
living with my second wife and myself.

She had a certain toughness too, coming from the

  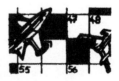

greatest hard wheat belts in the world. The only
daughter of a Shakespeare-reading real estate operator.
Though she had more love for her grandfather, a
pioneer physician in his one-room cabin 17 miles northwest of the town. I think this infatuation turned her on to
older men, living now, I gather, with someone twice
her age. She was something of a witch too, though I
never did see her spin off her skin. She spun mine
regularly enough. She had a great desire to expose the
pretention of pretending not to be pretentious and
therefore destroy the pretension by a general condition
of total candour in the mutual acknowledgement of all
pretension. She used to say that man would only be
altered by the over-throw of the human race or by
telepathy.

It was always a strenuous, but inspiring climb each
time I climbed into her cup-shaped crater. A vast
artesian reservoir beneath the surface. And each time
it was different. Never quite sure how it would be,
what I might find
furs
gold
silver
a Chinese sundial
a municipal campground
Some of her formations were so delicate and translucent
that a light placed behind brought out faint tints of pink
and tea rose. Often it was like entering three miles of
underground corridors. Spiralling through the great
entrance, over the rim, beginning about sundown, the
flights lasted at times up to 3 hours.

Living with her made me go in for a long-range effort
to develop a means of producing and maintaining a
controlled fusion reaction, which I thought if successful
could provide an infinite energy source. I had soon
lost most of my energy living with the two women, and
it had not taken long before I felt a prisoner in a snow-

padded fortress of Gothic Madonnas. Once one begins to doubt that 'good times' will last forever, then one becomes more cautious in one's decisions, demands will slow down, and emotions will taper off. I think the three of us soon came to realize that we were living in a desert where a flower is not a jewel, a tree is not a treasure. The green belts on the master plan were only sunbaked wastes. So, if you're having trouble deciding just where you want to go, we have a suggestion for you:

Go everywhere

The only problem is this: you still have to decide in what direction. Kidnap your wife. Just grab her and run. Getaway places that stretch right round the world. Places where the world will never find you. Places where you can find each other, all over again. And there you'll be. Listening to a million years of silence, or the sound of tomorrow in a discotheque. Pick up that phone. Kiss the lady. Pack a bag. Kick over the traces. No! She'll love you for it. Instead my wife was kidnapped by Nightripper. She left a note for both of us: Together you will rise to ever higher and higher platitudes. The correction I have made is a prerequisite to a resumption of healthy growth. Enjoy yourselves. Go West and turn right. Much love from the 'ANGUISHED'. P.S. I have left robe for you, please wear it and remember me. I shouted my no a little louder than normal. But I continued fantasizing in full colour: two lovely doxies and myself looking off into the middle distance from the rear deck of a Citroen Safari station wagon. At the same time I was moving away from the view that the structure of reality is a rigid framework, fixed in advance, and toward the view that it is a projection of human thought. I think finally it had been the girl's imagination, her fantasy world my second wife had grown jealous of. She certainly competed. Between them both my own fantasies became exhausted. Like those deprived of sleep, snatching dreams in catnaps. I was

more paranoid than I ever thought myself capable of.
I mean what does one do when there isn't a sexual
fantasy left to get a hardon for 18 miraculous hours?
I began having fantasies about animals.

The Disney fantasia is really a remarkable feat because
of difficulties encountered in deciding which end to
approach
half horse half alligator
mice and lizards with white coats blending in with the
dunes.
Always a persuasively exotic atmosphere whatever
creature imagined. I had to, above all, have the right
setting. Often I conjured up 30 acres of unspoiled
primitive beach
a semicircular recess in a great rock
an outdoor moated area
a cloistered walk
underground caverns with rare species of blind fish
a unique Aztec garden
formal boxwood gardens
Pioneer Mothers' Memorial forest
a triple-decker pulpit
Finnish Sauna baths and adjacent room with exercise
apparatus.
Lofty peaks and granite domes
A 1,000-foot-high volcanic cone, dotted by gnarled
ponderosa pine
The great dry seas of the moon
An effigy mound in the shape of an eagle
A concrete replica of Christopher Columbus' flag-ship.

At first it took time, but soon I was so accomplished
in arriving at the right setting that inside of 3
minutes I had automatically released a surge of new-
found delights. Inside of 3 minutes my body would idle
so smoothly that I thought it had stalled. But when I
stepped up the visual sense I'd feel the instant new power
response, feel in fact the new leap of power that was

131

mine to command at a touch of my fingers, and I
realised that something just short of a power-boosting
miracle had taken place within minutes. I got up to
83% more power potential. Thrilled to rocket starts
and takeoffs. Silence, knocks, pings, noises. The
strange neighing of the Unicorn. Perhaps the best.
That myth-cycle bag. At once sly, antic, playful,
imaginative hearty and at the same time hilarious and
thoroughly charming. The surprising manipulations
the unicorn's horn could do! A colourful and magnetic
image. Picturesque combination of Old World romance
and modern progress. And the others
white-tailed deer
racoon
fox
oppossum
muskrat
dove
turkey
and for further distraction I mixed them up
half oppossum half woman
Moth maid/human scorpion
water beetle woman/landlocked sockeye salmon with
human toes.

Soon while the women played out their fantasies with
me, with each other, I had a varied collection to choose
from. Unknown to either, they were winged, antler
headed fish-tailed creatures. Mammoths 12 feet tall
with tusks 6 feet long. By creating these I somehow
exhibited a remarkable adaptation to the peculiar
surroundings, resisting burial under the constantly
shifting roles.

Later I discovered my third wife had a thing about
unicorns, plus centaurs. Never very good at adapting
myself to either of these, she was fantastic. I realized
then that marriage with her could be a recreation in
previously unopened regions. Extensively developed

winter playgrounds, when she leaped over dome-shaped ground, neighing out for me to hunt her down. I eventually caught up with her near a hanging gorge, where spectacular panoramas unfolded as the snow dripped slowly off her. Entering her on that over-hanging gorge, in a snowdrift, was similar to being in an amphitheatre-like pit with terraced sides. Afterwards she had plans to call for retention of the wilderness character of the area. The ceremony was re-enacted at the exact hour 12:47 p. m. At least as long as the snow lasted. The unicorn days lasted. Only a few photos, a few memories are left to mark this era. She loved posing, painting her nipples with gold eyeshadow. Mine too. She dressed up, dressed down, making a more delightful access to impressive features.

Then I discovered she was on the needle, maybe Nightripper had initiated her. She'd close her eyes and say 'Dear me, I'm so depressed now. We must have some medicine. Who's got the spoon?' She fluttered to the other side of the room, then returned brandishing a syringe. 'Let's have a party, let's have a fix. I just don't feature getting strung out, I just don't dig it. Like there's no need for it, no need at all. You got a habit, you like your habit, it makes you feel so good, so very very good, you gotta feed your habit, you gotta be good to your habit, it's gonna be good to you. But you don't be good to your habit, then it's just gonna turn on you and be mean, real mean. It's gonna make you hurt, it's gonna give you such awful pain. And man, I don't like pain, no kind of pain. That's why I got a habit in the first place. You know that commercial we watch I always get a bang out of it. You know the one a bunch of women doing yoga, and this babe starts laying it on another babe about how good this yoghourt is for you. The second babe takes a mouthful. She swallows the stuff and closes her eyes. Then she says something that always makes me break up. She says

"Now this is inner peace." And every time I see that commercial I say, "yeah, inner peace," and I think about my habit.'

As for myself I soon arrived at the point when there were longings for themes that could be changed every 24 hours. An unusual series of deep loops. I knew I was still hungup from the rough equilateral triangle that appeared. A lurid vision of hell on earth. Wild orgies of possessed women who howled, shrieked and twitched like wolverines in heat. Keep up the good work you will never know how big this thing gets when there ain't nobody in it but one guy. Nefertair herself appeared wearing transparent linen and a vulture headdress. Even the most familiar dream trip will take on new excitement. Apparently I talked a lot in my sleep, and took to sleepwalking. He did not remember some of the most incriminating details until after he'd been hypnotized and shot with disquieting syrup. In more than 2 hours of withering close-order rituals he revealed a few joy boy kinetic tangles in his past, he said this harassment prevented him from getting a job, and also from engaging in dark urges on his custom-built electric bed.

It was suggested I find another chick and bring her home. I did find one, but didn't take her back. Might well have done, but the chick refused. Somehow she didn't see the situation as I described it: a natural bridge that would not only have an enormous and almost perfectly formed arch below, but also a curved surface above, giving the effect of a rainbow the three of us could slide over, under, and reach the other side at all angles, yet be almost a memorial of classic design. I think this chick saw it only as a grouping of petrified logs, herself in the middle. Gradually that affair fell below its lowest natural outlet and subsequently dried up. A remarkable paucity of imagination, I decided, even though she did have a pair of magnificent legs, beginning from the

navel. The way she walked you could tell she was really
a dignified white building with columned portico. She
really wanted something else. Out of the past. The
grandees and magnificoes, splendid entertainment,
ostentatious real estate, platoons of liveried flunkies,
titled sons and ocean-going yacht love nests. The lady
would rather be compared to an emerald. An emerald
as big as a board-room conference table adorned her
right hand. On her left was a tear-shaped stone that
could have originated only in the eye of a crocodile. By
the end emotions were so highly charged that we seemed
to be threatened by an irrevocable loss of cool.

My third wife and myself soon began experimenting in
a safety-padded instrument panel and twin padded sun
visors. Cozy, in-front-of-the-fireplace comforts: free
from leaks, draughts, rattles and flaps. I did, however,
wonder at the time if the imagination was getting
somewhat retarded simply because my information
processing and analysis were not efficient; that a
machine was needed economically and rapidly handling
my 'in-between' operations.

How did that marriage end? God knows, the further
removed from a situation the less objective I feel.
Misinterpretation of memory. The effects remembered,
but rarely the causes. My third wife's performances
combined simpering and savagery in a mercurial yet
carefully controlled characterization of neurotic
hysteria a la mode. At times our rows were sections
of reconstructed tracks with wooden rails pegged to
stone sleepers. The action usually ended at nightfall
with withdrawal. She locked herself up in the bathroom
with her syringe. He tittered after her as she headed
for the tub, bodystocking dangling from her wrist.
'Don't wear that thing in the bath, it might shrink and
you'll drown. ' The trouble was she fundamentally
had no sense of humour. So I was left giggling to myself,
laughter that soon turned sour in a chain-smoking night

135

filled with escape routes. Fantasies woven into further series of dioramas on the life and activities of our marriage. A bachelor's house - caustic revenge for an unhappy union where I devised an electric map of our battles, on which with the aid of 523 light bulbs the story of the 3-day battle is re-enacted. The lights controlled by 236 switches as the battle is explained. The reconciliations at first were o.k. but I became continually aware we were no closer to real calm than the eye of a hurricane, which I looked at from an air-conditioned cell of stucco and glass. I longed for some chemical change in the crisis. Crisis upon crisis. Door-banging, drawer-slamming fights as intricate as Chinese puzzles. When the bullets start whizzing around my head I like to think I get the coolest. I pictured myself as the crime fighter, standing alone against the Mongol hordes. But hard to feel this the next morning when yesterday's truths become today's half-truths, and high heroics suddenly seem theatrics.

And this ridiculous drama now? Pursuing my first X-wife, or rather being pursued. Who was chasing who I had forgotten. Perhaps I should put a call through and ask them? But I remembered the penalty for making an obscene or harassing call (including those where the caller remains silent) could be as much as a year in the pokey and $1,000 fine. The simplest decisions now meet extensive delays. I believe the record is clear as to which side has gone the extra mile in this drama, now is the time for the other side to respond. A city can be a jungle, giving no hint of the terror stalking in the darkness. Only when a private citizen raises his voice to help the police may light pierce the wall of the wild. He invited her into his motel room in the politest way imaginable - and snuffed out her life while she was still thinking what a great guy he was.

I went outside, and again looked through the keyhole.

Inlets of spectacular silver presented an ever-changing vista. I recognized that tight fitting dress. I had bought it for her birthday, soon after her father had preached one of his sermons about his daughters: 'They're as solid as those trees out there 'n they don't smoke, or drink, and the others at least married fine boys.' And so on, the usual stuff, a lot of apple pie and motherhood, going on to denounce the banks and utilities, and the rich on Wall Street who don't pay their taxes, and his enemies 'Who drink tea at the country club with their little fingers stubbed straight up, and never do a darn thing worthwhile.' While I stood there and scrutinized the floor, hoping I'd find another pin. During one of his interminable speeches I had picked up a pin, and neatly placed it on a little table next to him. I think he actually liked having me around. I gave him an umbrella in which to legitimatize his pathology, act out his problems and be rewarded for it.

Reward? Yes perhaps that's what was needed right then as I watched my first wife bend like a silver tinsel Christmas tree branch. At no other place was there such a feeling of time displaced. And I wanted her as I had never wanted her before. To enter her from that angle. Have her then split. A gesture. Some sign. But the only sign at that moment was the growing awareness of myself outside in a hot night rising in majestic isolation. Blood creating large numbers of humming-birds that flocked into my head.

Now that these dire events have you all shook up how can you resist? Move in on them, judo throw him, rally from blows that would kayo ordinary mortals. Ever in trouble? You bet he is. But he can dish it out as well as take it. As for instance his eerie energies surge out in a flow of furious force. O.K. so don't spare the horses you know what to do. To the attack! With fists and knuckles, super weapons and raw courage he hurls himself at a foe whose very touch means instant destruction. Does he hesitate? Dilly-dally? Perish forbid. And my first wife - the claw-happy fighter who relishes a bang-up rock-em sock-em rhubarb - would naturally be turned on by my brute force, the display of hitting him so fast and hard that he'd think he was being battered by a human triphammer. So locked in Titanic struggle the two hate-full brutes have been trading battering blows. And her eyes pop out at the sight of her fallen lover, who she steps over and falls sobbing into X-husband's arms, submissive to my awesome power.

Seeing him approach the door, I flattened myself against the wall as he emerged. 'It's all right honey there's no one here - who did you think...' The door closed. Low voices. Silence. The heat. The humming-blood turned cold. Exhausted again I went back to my room. Onto the bed.

I dreamed of a lake 500 feet deep where I lost my boots. Convinced that sly fink in the next room had taken them, I hunted him down in a city of flowering magnolias, picturesque lakes and bayons, winding drives, stately ante bellum houses, and through imposing government buildings that changed into a gracious frame house held together by white oak pegs, where my wife stood, holding the boots, brightly polished, with silver laces, which she handed me, together with an etched-glass candle lamp, and led me first to an awesome round bed with black satin sheets, and to a trapeze, where she swung in voluptuous positions.

I woke up in a cold sweat. What was real, what wasn't? All merged into an immense interior region. Somehow, somewhere there ought to be unusual flood-light illumination. My mind was a crucible containing a constantly burning fire. A row of musical stalactites surrounding. Electrically charged. The night. Days

were nights. Dreams were reality. Reality seen
through a rear-view mirror. No sense of time. Tombs
of solid masonry 100 or more feet long and 4 tiers high.
Winding stairs and wrought iron balustrade. A dome
with many coloured panes of glass through which I saw
nothing. Heard nothing. Felt nothing. Similar to when
I lay in an operating room. Ventilated by unscreened
open windows, but there at least I had seen the entrance
of pigeon excreta, even though I felt the pigeon
droppings were the last I would see of the world. But
kept my cool. Contrary to now when I could so easily
flip. No one any the wiser. And death? There is no
death. But if you kill yourself you displease the Great
Spirits and you may be reincarnated as a worm. Well
why not - a worm's life is better than this. Go back
to sleep. Go on with the game. The chase. The kill.
Get the gun loaded. Terror spread when a fiend struck
silently and then slipped away in the dark. Behind him
the bloodthirsty psychopath left a trail of ghastly
skulls - a trail that led the police exactly nowhere.

The current lull must be regarded only as a time of
repair and rebuilding by the enemy before its next
attack. Ah yes certainly no dream that. This. The pit
enclosed. All the gore and thunder of a standard
western. A welcome relief from the comparatively
barren surroundings. Why not admit it. Yes. What is
it you're selling? The process of the game. You can't
get blood out of turnip so stop thinking you are nursing
a hot potato. My decision is final, firm and not subject
to further consideration. What decision? Take a lie
detector test to determine whether these are the facts.
What facts - what decision? To weigh, measure,
reassess every move. Squeeze out that last ounce of
juice? That the future may learn from the past.
Bullshit. You've met what you consider defeat and you're
on the threshold of disillusionment. Then the worst
thing I can do is throw cold water on your expectations.

He sounds like a man in panic.

Don't be an eyeglass pusher-upper. Non-slide eye-
frames. Discover the comfort of glasses that hug
your head, stay in place...thanks to a new spring hinge
that eliminates nagging nose push ups. Bend, shake or
nod your head. The no-slide frame never moves. Foam
glass insulation. The world coinciding with something
inside my ear. A gleaming stainless steel arc.
Spanish moss-hung trees. A new system of fluorescent
lighting, making everything 325 times brighter than
the moon. Two million specimens of multi-coloured
insects expanding above and below me. Ranks of
finlike formations rear into spires. Semi-arid desires
alternate with isolate needs.

The general orientation and interpretation of the area?
A bird without a proper band and life-time number is
a nonparticipant, a nothing-bird like a hood whose
fingerprints never made the files of the F.B.I. Then
pack your bags, leave a note under their door: Hurry
I'm missing you. Please contact me would like to know
how you are. Or better still: Greetings to my
Fingelheimer, my Sugar Bunny Doonk, my wife - the
Rock of Gibraltar, and the dearest of them all, my
Mother-in-Law for a wonderful year. Only 118 more to
go. May Life Be An Eternal Snowflake. Love - The
Boss. Wouldn't that be artificially elevating the
situation? Why don't I just split right away? In fact get
to the border, never return - what use has this country,
I for it, it for me? Don't go around the barn go directly
in. What in the world are you waiting for? How many
more tomorrows are you going to wait for the trip you've
been putting off? And off. And off. Give yourself no
more gall stones. Don't put it off a minute longer, we
can have your head in the clouds the day after you make
up your mind like maybe tomorrow. Now where exactly
is the power centre? The power centre, a man for all
crisis was at that moment walking up and down in a

motel room, with remarkable ease and sense of blood
lust, or was he in fact the tormented victim of a
national policy and a command system that placed him
unprepared in such awful jeopardy? Very well I shall
not be responsible for the consequences.

I left no note, and just as I drove out of the car port
she opened the door, barefoot and wearing a yellow
kimona with Chinese characters, quotations from
Chairman Mao. Her eyelashes were still in the drawer,
which I noted as being highly unusual, why she wore
those just to go to the mailbox. I continued
manoeuvering their Buick, while watching her get
nearer. What could I do, open the door, drag her in?
Confused, undecided I waited. Watch out for that camera
she has. The secret agent movie-shot looks like a
movie camera turns into a cap firing machine gun.
There were several shots as I turned the corner, and
the Buick skidded into the soft shoulder. So that's it
she's really out to kill me! For a change this is a
serious situation.

> Nude Divorcee and the Camera Clue
> A Blonde, A Guy and A Gun
> A fatal combination that could spell murder!

They were bearing down on me in the Chevy. She
had the window open. I saw her polaroid swinger
camera. Evidence needed? Stealing their car? And
there he was, leaning over the steering wheel, no doubt
imagining he was Lieutenant Colonel Custer in his
paywagon. He was wearing one of those very expensive,
hand-embroidered Philippine peek-aboo evening shirts.
Beneath the pale-peach voile, with its cutouts, was
clearly visible a heavy white knit undershirt. What
bugged me was that he seemed so typical. I mean it
would be different if he'd been one of those always
behind-the-eight-ball types, but he was obviously as
normal as normal can be. With, no doubt, a Ph.D. in

141

chocolate icecream. And oh how great she looked, half
hanging out of the window, her breasts swinging under
the camera. Organized womanhood. Women's Lib
Chick. The hand that refuses to rock the cradle. We know
she's good looking - with elegant custom-contoured
seat. And a modern floor shift. Plus lots of head, leg
and shoulder, a panoramic front made of laminated
safety glass. And a padded dash. And extra large blade
drums. Tears were seen welling in his eyes. I think
it was sweat - but it was a great feeling - maybe it
was tears.

I bent over the wheel, stepped up the gas. With such
terrific pressure on my back it was as if I had caused
a volcanic vent through which great globules of lava
were blown high into the air and with the ashes, cinders
fall to earth, piling around the vent in a conical hill.
Admit you are getting tired of the whole works. But
something else might happen. What grotesque shape their
thoughts? The razor-sharp edges of their plans? Their
organizational chart like a wiring diagram for a
perpetual-motion machine. And my own? At this stage
extreme caution must be exercized. Despite his dearth
of personal principles, but with his own twist. Her act
of aiming the gun was obviously a graphic illustration of
the way in which her madness, warped and tilted, had
built up. I no longer saw her mother's face there, but
her father's. That glint of satisfaction in his eyes while
admitting that one of the finest moments of his day was
his 11 p.m. massage administered while watching some
guest attempting to master the stone maze on his 500-
acre property. The maze contained 1,680 feet of
passageway, with brick walls running from 6 to 8 feet
in height, landscaping was a backdrop of melancholy
trees. He considered the maze 'an aesthetic experience,
a symbol in a world so caught up with scientific
rationalism it doesn't know where it's going. You can't
get to the centre of a maze by going straight for you

have to be indirect. The way to attain something is to go away from it. The maze is a spiritual truth.' He could make it to the centre in 5 minutes. For the uninitiated, like myself, it could take hours of trial and error. And he knows the psychology of handling cows - you start the cows slow and then accelerate as they get near the pen. Like father, like daughter.

Maybe the charge in the divorce proceedings had not been far off the mark. Extreme cruelty. That I had treated her in such a way as to injure health and endanger reason. Certainly she blamed me for her miscarriage, even though she was secretly relieved. She hated the idea of getting fat. Loathed my fantasies of her suckling a baby as well as myself. The whole image, in fact, of The Mother. Besides she was quite convinced it would have been a monster or the messiah. No in-betweens for her. For myself I must admit it was hard forgoing the picture of an 18th century Neapolitan Nativity scene. She had conceived in a small park, under some picnic tables, near a shelter house. I remember the afternoon vividly. It was the second time we had made it, the first in the mineral baths, already described.

Undulating fields of wheat touched the horizon. Her hair smelling of magnolia. Steady hum of freeway traffic. For some reason, while lying on her, I saw the image of mother standing on a wide veranda over-looking a garden of period flowers and herbs. From what underground reservoir this memory came I had no idea. Anyway it left me feeling profoundly happy. So much so I got a hard on a second time and made a fantastic trip right through the garden, the flowers, herbs etc. and exploded on the veranda. That was when she conceived, at least she said it was, and felt a great disappointment. The setting, somehow, was not at all appropriate. I tried convincing her that for a messiah it couldn't have been better. 'A monster - monster,'

143

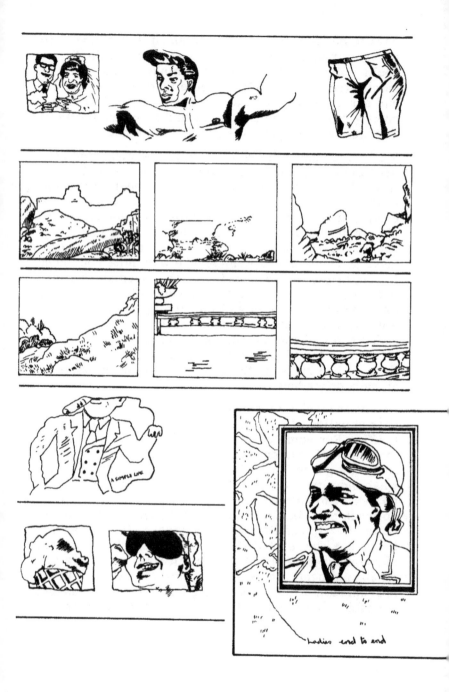

she screamed, hitting me around the head and
shoulders later, after we had been taken back to the
family estate, the actual day of our wedding. She made
it out to be as if I had pulled some kind of stunt. The
larger she grew the more outraged she became. I tried
reassuring her that it might not have been at the picnic
area at all. But in some resplendent
wildflower gardens
an enclosed gondola lift
an enchanted mesa 430 feet above surrounding plains
beside frozen blue lakes high above a valley floor
a rolling plain dotted with isolated mountain ranges
making it the second time while a tom-tom echoed a
weird tattoo as a writhing dancer pleaded for rain.
Snow-banked forests
Fountain basins lined with masses of cave onyx
resembling lily pads
Tall graceful stalagmites formed like totem poles.
Snow white glistening dunes that we rose with 10 to 40
feet above the valley floor, where the dry winds
evaporate the lake and whirled the crystallized gypsum
particles into the surrounding area. Our bodies, the
dunes ever changing.
Sparsely covered with plant growth at the fringes.
A glass-enclosed lobby
A sandstone building of neoclassic design with a golden
dome 50 feet in diameter where I spread her thighs out.
An Indian burial pit
A natural limestone building 220 feet long with twin
towers, 141 feet high. Bavarian stained-glass windows
imported from Munich, where she stood, leaned out
and I took her there with the sun dividing us up into
luminous particles that spread out and touched the
broad fertile valleys below.
Or even in the centre of her father's stone maze.

'It'll be a monster goddamit what else in that
picnicking dump - and it'll have a coke bottle for a

head you'll see.' She screamed. Like her father I
suppose she wants style, a smooth efficient operator
with a horror of small errors. Once during the summer,
a picnic went badly. No more picnics he told his wife.
And during a banquet he spilled soup on his sleeve, no
more soup at these things, he decreed.

Memories. Images. They end up as a kind of emotional
fishhook, snagged in the mind. Not wholly explicable,
but impossible to dislodge. Wrap them up. Move on.
Tunnel under the situation. Come up behind them and
POW. It's the only way, hit them straight on, or the
s. o. b. s. will clobber you every time. Face the
situation as it is. He has long borne the aura of power,
carefully contained but ready for instant action. Above
all while we have the power, we must aim at confronting
the enemy directly. We can win every such confrontation.
Like a practised surfer, he was balanced carefully in
the curl, in control of his board and in no apparent
danger of a wipe-out. I walk tall. I do my thing. They
try to break you. They won't break me.

In front I could see blue grey basaltic columns, up to
60 feet tall, fitted together into organ pipes, making a
sheer 300-foot wall. Cathedrals to silence I longed to
see as the eagle sees them. And behind me? Yes still
dutifully following. I couldn't see her face. Only the
camera. Hold one. Handle it. Get it into shooting
position. Note how remarkably well-balanced it is.
Look through the precise functionally located controls.
Feel the satin-smooth chrome, the richly grained
leather. His face took up at least half of the rear-view
mirror. Obviously the type who keeps a punching bag in
his room and every once in a while beats the hell out of
it. At the same time possessed of a rich musical
heritage enjoying, no doubt, playing his cello to his
mother's violin accompaniment. Urbane, tall, affable
and attractive. Knew his ABCs when he was 2, able to
recite all the nursery rhymes. Went to school in his

146

little red Buster Brown suit, or dressed like a cowboy, wearing his father's Stetson. Most of his life spent fiercely appearing what he isn't and vice versa. Having tantrums about stories which say he has tantrums. Trying to perpetuate the myths that he had a great-great grandfather who died at the Alamo, that he isn't persistently overweight. And two stories erected of his birthplace and his boyhood home, both looking less like what they were than what he probably wished they had been: glassed, aluminized, air-conditioned, painted, and manicured.

Pray watch the actions of the Enemy, and if they incline to retreat or advance, harass their Rear and Flanks... On the other hand I could treat them with humanity... No. Get rid of them, lose them somehow. Journey on alone? Alone. Making some trip to some place with only memories to deal with, fight with? Flipping out finally in their Buick in some deserted town. Too wet for anyone to hang out. He is coasting. He is in trouble. He is taking aspirin for relief when he should be taking something stronger for a cure. He needs long-range vision, not a daily balance sheet. Disguise myself, go under a John Doe, and pursue them. Shave my head (always a leaning towards the monastic). His close-cropped skull and impassive features give him the forbidding countenance of a Japanese warlord. Difficult. When one thinks about it. Impossible to make a new life when a man lives with the thought that his baby footprints are in the records of the state, that his fingerprints are on file with the FBI, and that much of his private life, probably including a psychological report, resides in the files of his credit bureau:

> Attitude towards regulations - violates all of them
> Honesty - needs watching
> Appearance - repulsive
> Courtesy - seldom if ever polite

No disguise then. Retreat. To where? A choice.

There's a winter home for the world's last flock of
wild whooping cranes
or a place where only deer, coyotes, foxes and the
collard peccary roam.
Somewhere untouched by residential sprawl. A vast
and lonely tract of sand and scrub. Shifting dunes that
support only sunflowers, a little grass and a low-growing
species of pea. But why rough it? Retire to a 10-room
Spanish-style villa on a 75-foot cliff overlooking the
Pacific. Shielded from the road by a stand of eucalyptus
trees. Security guaranteed by 1,500 ft. of fencing and
several observation posts constructed in the same time-
roofed style as the villa's main buildings. Spotlights
installed on the bluff to illuminate the ocean at night.
The alarms are tripped by various means - metallic
foil on windows, ultrasonic waves, photoelectric beams -
and connected by telephone wire to a central panel at
police headquarters. But his X-wife had joined a group
of Women Against War Toys, and marched to the
beach below his clifftop castle and constructed an edifice
of their own: a sand castle of peace.

At once he had lost his target, his chief issue, his
psychological motivation, his under-dog aura and his
strategy. Instead of a wild slugging match, he faced
a methodical and joyless duel. The argument with
himself. Confront that then. Finally that's where it's
at. Living in balance like a moose population with
predatory wolves. Where the imagination floats in
caves with sightless crawfish. Where the iniative?
That sense of being ready for anything, when you feel
like you can lick anybody, or pull off any kind of job?
The problem, of course, is that at times he gets so
enthusiastic about his fictionalized images that he
isolates himself from fact. And the fact is they are out
to kill. Or is that fantasy too? Like a speed freak I'll
soon get to the point of seeing them in the trees with
cameras. Slow down. See what happens. Get out,

shake hands, tell them it's getting a drag: Let's work
and reason together. Let us share and trust. Here is
my Liquidation /Reinvestment Principle:

> The choice of three separate plans designed to meet
> our specific needs
>
> A selection of high performances
>
> The flexibility to change from one recommended
> plan to another without cost to the energy
>
> The right to withdraw from each other's company
> at any time
>
> The freedom to move

Today's man of action speaks his mind, moving to
make his mark on a dozen tired computers, he wants
them to indulge in self-interrogation: 'What are we
attempting to do?'
How would we measure success?
What kind of world are we trying to bring about?
The computer previously programmed with all the
necessary formulas, patterns of responses, will
quickly calculate all the various stresses and forces
involved and tell whether the plan will hurt. Torn yet
relieved by successive shocks he will murmur the
healing formula of self-acceptance 'It is I,' overriding
feelings of shame and the dread of retribution
particularly in the form of castration. 'Only small
numbers of the emotionally ill can be reached by any
one method,' says Manhattan psychotherapist S (For
Samuel?) who is not an analyst but whose orientation
is Freudian. This is a lesson that, by chastening the
defensive heirs of Freud who would admit no one else
to their club, and by vastly expanding the quest for
psychiatry's ultimate consumer: the man who is out of
harmony with himself and with his wife. But who or
what is 'Btfsplkian'? Please set me straight I may not
sleep for fear of it turning up in D.C. in some Jekyll
guise. 'Can Peaches overhaul the Laius reaction?'
But she's no activist except for her spirited championing

of life in the afternoon and Mr. Sam and the long slack season. A rounding bottom indicates that after a long decline father figures have finally sold out. They seem positively euphoric about their mission. The whole place pretty freed up, satanism and embroidery are the girls' thing, and the men are dressed up when they don't go around in zipper fragments. Even Batman in Fatigues is caught up in the mood: 'I walk to work, I camp in the house, I sleep with the Manual on the Mafia, or just lie with the Economic Wringer on a dune buggy.' Will it fit into your organization?

My father-in-law came into focus. The day he stood in his study, hands in his pockets, with the beauty of the summer rose garden showing through the French doors, when he gathered his thoughts about his delinquent son-in-law, and with a few modifications he again quoted from the Bible: 'I brought you into a plentiful home, to eat the fruit thereof and the goodness thereof; but when ye entered, ye defiled my home, and made mine heritage an abomination.' 'And what have you done to my daughter - why you have raided an exotic garden and left only a pale hothouse flower, and until you can improve and correct your behaviour we are going to be confronted with unpleasant situations...we can't correct it overnight, but we are trying at this end of the line as best we can - I realize the days of the stick and carrot are gone, and that your generation needs opportunity for impact...' He paused to recharge 'but let's face it your marriage has to be judged a colossal failure.' His weathered face was lined with new arroyos and his hair curled whitely over his collar like Senator Claghorn's, but there was no mistaking his manner. He dominated every room he entered, looming over his listeners like a huge bird, booming his homespun dialectic, gesturing expansively with arms and head and torso. He went on and told the old story of the blind Indians who tried to describe an elephant. One man felt the trunk and said the elephant was snakelike, another felt a leg and said it resembled a tree. My answer: Experiments may be on the verge of a technical breakthrough that will render the current experience obsolete. And his reply: 'one concludes from what is not being done that there is no real commitment in this effort other than verbal.'

I can't remember much else of the dialogue, except we ended up talking about how careful one has to be not to be impaled on the wicked fin of a hooked catfish. Later that same day a walk with my Mother-in-Law over the manicured gardens. The night in her car dismissed, as if nothing had happened between us. A game I soon adapted to amazingly quickly. Though at times living with this family seemed an immense indoor swimming pool making me feel like an extra in a home movie. Their endless talk of what they had done. The stories of his youthful trip in quest of a fortune. Every night, apparently, he had buried his wallet and the $27 in it under the desert sands for fear it would be stolen when he was asleep. The perverse pleasure he took in making his wife serve him a plate of pork and beans, much to her embarrassment. To purge herself, I guess, she took me aside and said things like: 'I want there to be a lot of life here - see those windows that face onto the courtyard well that's going to be a stable, won't it be nice to have horses' heads protruding out of the windows?' She, of course, most of the time figures there was, or ought to be, more to life.

Herewith some glum disclosures about what it means to succeed in an affluent society: 'By the time you have finished paying for the simple necessities like a self-cleaning oven and jaunts like a weekend to our No. 3 home there's simply nothing left over for plain fun.' 'If I've been sick and stay at home in the morning I might have lunch (his chauffeur delivers a meat sandwich, a salad and a thermos of milk) and then go

151

out and even buy a razor blade, just that makes me feel better.' ('My wife must eat a buck and half a day'.) He doesn't believe in postponing things: 'How would you feel if the Russians sent something over and you hadn't had a vacation that year?' After considerable reckoning they judged that their gerbil consumes 29c worth of sunflower seeds every two weeks. But she compensates by doing all the housework, she happens to have a compulsive need to vacuum. She accidentally cut off an inch of Bu-Bu's tail (medical bill $50). To console her he bought her a Rudi Gernreich wool knit ($70). He envisions the cost of living as a never-ending spiral. He drinks Volpe meade, dyes his hair, and insists that regular doses of olive oil have kept him from the whole urban affairs-welfare-face relations complex. She talked of all this in an alto-register voice, well-bred and well-couched, while she sipped vodka-on-the-rocks. 'Not that I think I am terribly good at things - but something's there and if it doesn't get some exposure then there's the terrible empty feeling of going down the drain.' I learned that what she really wanted was to reappear perennially on the list of the world's 10 best-dressed women. To be beautiful and elegant and have a brain and a workable wit. Have best friends like Rudolf Nureyev and Dame Margot Fonteyn and Truman Capote. The mobility to join friends for capricious last minute jaunts to Africa and Mexico. Meanwhile she had to be satisfied with staying at their No. 1 home this year and dine off haggis from Scotland and caviar from Iran. While he worked alone in the little study next to the of office, going over his papers, while his stereo blared Kostelanetz or the score from Victory at Sea. Often he sat discouraged in his rumpled underwear, watching television, attempting to ignore that the gardens were signalling the season he loved to spend down on the ranch watching the new life cycle begin. At such times he emphasized the fact that he was not a blooded

patrician just a striver who has acted out the middle-
class dream. 'I earned my money didn't inherit it,'
he'd shout at the three of us. 'I do the very best I
know how and if the end brings me out all right, what
is said against me won't amount to anything. If the end
brings me out wrong, 10 angels swearing I was right
would make no difference.' Satisfied with the guilty
looks that passed across our faces, he'd start lifting
his hand to his forehead as if brushing away a droplet
of sweat, then stop the motion, bring his hand down,
and stare with a glazed expression at the tube. Such
moments as these I actually felt pity for him, perhaps
recognizing a slight affinity. The thing of drifting from
the insomniac sack to play Television Russian
Roulette. A mentally hazardous game, but easy to
play. Push the 'on' button, bravely twirl the plastic
channel-selecting wheel and fatalistically watch
whatever film materializes. Usually a bouquet of
commercials: beer, bad breath, athlete's foot, cake
mix, dog food and hair spray. And there he was,
slumped in his underwear. Nothing innocent about him,
the thin cigar, the grim scowl when offering some
dire pronouncement, the roguish smile when light-
hearted, made him easy to caricature, easy to suspect
of ulterior motives. Whatever he did, he was well aware
that he was a man leaning into stiffer gales of challenge
than any of us. And if depressed he would try to
convince that it was not his fault or responsibility. The
facts of his life collected and fed to the computer. In
addition to such basics as his name, address, bank
references, marital status and bill-paying habits, his
debts and how he pays them are recorded. He never
physically abuses his wife, and he's a good provider
'I want you to be happy, here's some money go buy
yourself a mink stole or something.' Behind his
saturnine face and his passionless blue grey eyes, can
be a warm and even a lovable man for those who acquire
the taste. But he is a tough man, shrewd and self-

assured, standing there beside the backyard barbecue pit, swathed in an apron and holding a Manhattan on the rocks as he contemplates his prized swimming pool. Or sitting out on the terrace with a bourbon in one hand and a BB gun in the other to shoo the squirrels away from the seeds he put out for the birds. Much of the time he was like a hairy, double-jawed grasshopper, a normal grasshopper, evenly dispersed and alone. Then suddenly and at unpredictable intervals he turns into a mob, blackening the skies like a tornado. The manic change in his personality apparently triggered by some violent alteration in the household, or sharp fluctuations in temperature or humidity or the stock market. At such times he developed a voracious appetite. But his wife continued believing in 'give him grits and a hamburger and he's happy. ' His substantive approach on most issues was cautious. Instinct his radar, calculation his principal weapon.

I turned down his offer of working as a salesman for his ballpoint pens, and proved in front of him that they were easily breakable. He looked and sounded not unlike Hitler but without the charm - he began to shriek insults in order to head me off, and succeeded for by then my mission was accomplished. I had enticed the cuckoo to sing its song, and the melody lingered on. I expected no reciprocity from my wife or Mother-in-Law. The essential difficulty of my position was that I had to avoid, at all costs, allowing the other side to gain the impression that I was withdrawing out of weakness. However I had a reasonable expectation that the pattern (their responses to my initiatives) would change, and if it didn't that would tell me something too, when the record of those months would become clear in the future it would be seen that I was negotiating in good faith and was ready to offer them a fair deal. Sadly enough, I guess, the true picture I left was a fleeting presence, a blurred picture, a voiceless phantom. As for my father-in-law, when viewed from a distance, he always seemed to turn to celluloid. One dimension yet spread out on a screen; the marks on his face appeared to have come not so much from the real collisions of life as from the newspapers that surrounded him. And though he heatedly denied his wife's remark that he consulted the stars before making any decision, he did at the odd hour of ten past midnight on his birthday plant a 19-inch-high Japanese bonsai tree, a book on Practical Bonsai for Beginners open in front of him as he knelt digging. 'He changes into the most decrepit clothes you ever saw and gets into his garden. He loves getting dirt under his fingernails.'

I slowed down. Where had they got to? A deserted freeway. During the time of 'peace' the 'enemy' prepares the way for attack and internal disruption. Often a man's main opposition is on his doorstep. I am not the first prophet without honour at home. The hard-lined face seemed to take on years of universal torture, and the voice never lost its special craggy heroism. An electric language that is in touch with the churning guts and sweaty pores of the real world. One cannot help but suspect some sinister machination or to put it in plainer terms, the whole thing smells of a fix. He looked at his boots the casual, crushable boot, glove-soft leather specially tanned to take a long life of comfortable use and abuse.

Shortly, after a concealed change of costume disdaining dangers he zeros in on his human targets. Like a wounded buffalo he crouches, shaking his head to clear it. Like a man in a cataleptic state he cannot speak, he cannot move, he suffers no pain, and yet he is perfectly conscious of everything that is going on about him. Here it is distinctly seen how the external manifestation of the act, something really quite secondary, overcomes what is essential. Reactions of this kind are characteristic and suffice secondary states of feeble-mindedness. Make no mistake about it he's strumming a real gut chord.

He seems to be living in kind of lobotomized euphoria. One realizes that his larger suffering is remorse of conscience, a troubled unremitting scrutiny of the shortcomings of his own character. His style is tense, elliptic, introspective. It mirrors a high speed mind - an internal dialogue, a constant contrapuntal debate waged between his thoughts and his mind. My conclusions are plain. I will not surrender. I do not wish to enlarge the conflict. I desire peaceful settlement and talks. He wandered pensively into the woods, his Secret Service men shadowing him at a respectful distance as he began the lonely job of deciding. His fundamental intention was to thrust himself above the hurly-burly of debate onto some rarefied plane where only posterity - and a far-off posterity at that - would be fit to judge him. 'After all,' remarked one Free Democrat 'isn't it nicer to die in the arms of your lover than out in the cold?' Pompeianism suited many a Fifties liberal, with his passive sense of impending catastrophe and his culturally induced impotence in the face of Joe McCarthy and Curtis LeMay (Q. What did you do in the Great War Daddy? A. I sat down in an orderly manner, baby, ate some larks' tongues and waited for the ash.)

The time has come to call a halt to this Theatre of the Absurd, to examine the motivation of the authors of the absurdity and challenge the star players. Let me now, as they say in court, connect up with the current scene. You will not hear disquisitions in the manner of William Graham Sumner or Friedrich Hayek on the legitimacy and functionalism of privilege. Such palaver would be thought only boring. Now a Geiger Counter detects Freudian signs of suppressed guilt

156

feeling. Oh God, he cried, I wish I could be in my own pad like in Malibu, sitting on the deck, drink in one hand, my chick on the other, and listening to the surf fall. But he'd gone that route enough times to have pained memories 'Blah, blah blah. Get stiff. Grab a shower. Take a plane. Blah, blah, blah! As he moved along the chit-chat-and-canape circuit last week in his polka-dot shirt, Levis and sneakers, he seemed more a displaced mountain man than...

But the scene now. Your Horoscope for Today. Now at last you can win over that man who seems indifferent to your charms. Attract him by showing new facets of your personality. Signs favour a casual shopping trip together. Ask his opinion on a see-through body shirt. Try on seductively feminine crepe pajamas.

He wanted food, warmth, but most of all slippers, light coats and a cigarette. A comfortable garb. He moved darkness like a man hiking a black sea. It was five o'clock out of the car and Sunday morning, and although the public was led to believe the nude bride in the bath had died accidentally, the police knew otherwise. She was slain at 'A', dragged to point 'B', then to spot at far left (X) where body was found. Arrows show killer's escape path. Circles mark his footprints in the mud. He lived on discarded fruit and left proof of self-decay.

He set the hour of road a mile and half south. Behind a hedgerow for a short distance his evening meal remained at right angles to the road. He stripped nude and hacked his victim's head near a decaying wire fence. A patrolling reserve instrument the killer used.

Mystery of the Missing Corpse Detectives were puzzled until a faint odour provided a lead.

Feel so good I'll treat myself to a Drive-In-Movie.

As darkness shrouds the land and the silver screen leap to life. But my mind's full of Romantic thoughts all I know is I've got a burning desire to kiss that girl in the next car. I can't fight it. Underfoot the earth shudders, groans. As dirt and rock slide wide apart. Keep calm, sure that's a girl screaming, but you don't have to play hero all the time! Give somebody else a chance to be the Glory Boy. Still, it wouldn't take much energy just to open one eye to peep at what's going on. And now that I'm more like my true self again. O-oh here comes that Emotional charge in me again.

A man with a long face, wide ears, and a crooked mouth got out of his car. There was an odd glittering expression in his eyes, and a .32 calibre revolver in his right hand. As he approached the couple in the car, he raised the weapon, squinted briefly along its barrel and pressed the trigger.

He seized the shrieking woman by the arm and dragged her back to his car. Suddenly she wrenched herself away from him, and in utter desperation tried to crawl beneath the Buick. Her assailant pulled her from beneath the car and threw her into the front seat. Then he jumped in beside her, stepped on the accelerator and drove off.

Batgirl may fight like a male, but her thinking is strictly female.

Missing three days the lovely blonde was found nude and ravished in a lonely lane. Police needed a clue, and they soon unearthed an odd one.

Was he destined for flophouses, transient hotels, isolated rural areas and other nooks where people could be conceivably missed and the census never catches up. In 1890 the federal inquisitors asked no fewer than 470 questions. 'If there are any idiots living in the house, what is their head size (small,

large, or natural)?' 'Has the origin of this child been respectable?' 'Is this resident habitually intemperate, or tramp, or syphilitic?'

Muscle and mercy
Time out for familiar issues
Active, visible and accountable.

Why did he long for her laughter? A corroboree of chuckles, whinnies and convulsions and her chatter about hand-me-down clothes, daytime naps, gardening and sibling rivalry ('Who gets the fruit cocktail with the lone cherry on top?') chewing gum, home barbering and the ides of March. 'If a woman is ever to have an affair it will be in March, psychologically, it is the perfect month. The bowling tournaments are over, the white sales on bedding are past. Your chest cold has stabilized and the Avon Lady is beginning to look like Tom Jones.' And at times she seems preoccupied as if she smelled something burning in the oven rather than in her. At another it is daytime soap opera as she tersely barks 'I'm trying to clean you out of me.' And yet again addicted to cigarette burns on her chest, black leather lingerie on her body, and shoes with stiletto heels on her feet, she howled, screamed and moaned without once stepping that half-inch over into the ludicrous.

We've made it this far together and we'll finish it together. He climbed behind the wheel and drove off cross-country rousing deer from the live-oak thickets. Palm trees here and there and lots of lush heavy vegetation. A sky-scraper rises right out of a parking lot right next to a row of 1930 bungalows.

The footprints suggesting a woman had been on the scene opened the door wide to a multitude of speculations as to the motive for the fatal assault.

The investigators speculated as to whether it was the woman who had strewn the victim's clothing along the highway. There was also conjecture as to whether the woman had been an active participant or merely a spectator to the sadistic stripping of the victim and leaving him to freeze to death in the night. What drove the West Wild was ladies named Millie Hipps, Mattie Silks, Mammy Pleasant, Madame Moustache. Lurline Monte Verdie and Silver Dollar.

He saw only her long chiffon scarf and high-tongued cranberry leather boots vanish into the car. And her loverboy with shaped sideburns and iridescent orange mock turtleneck under a shaped blue sports jacket and checked continental pants. All week long he might wear grey and black, but to go to the delicatessen on Sunday night he dresses as if he was going to the track, like a hipster moving to a beat slightly less groovy than the bossa nova, walking slowly, chewing on a cigar like he has really made it BIG. His eyes are wintry; the rare smile that bends his straight mouth is the sort of rupture that starts avalanches. He is a pusher-up and a weight lifter, a methodical schedule of calisthenics (20 pushups, 20 sit-ups and 40 jumping jacks each morning) a user of nothing more addictive than prune juice. He loves to hear her talk after attending a rap session of the women's Liberation with the express purpose of raising consciousness. 'Did you realize that the number of abortions actually exceeds the number of American soldiers killed in Viet Nam?' Sporting her button bearing the nickname of Uppity women. A really active woman liberator can go to a meeting every night raising consciousness one evening and funds the next. 'Women have got jobs as jockeys, steamship yeomen and telephone switchmen, which were formerly denied them. Soon I feel we can expect legions of female firemen, airline pilots, sanitation men and front-line soldiers (although Margaret Mead thinks that they would be too fierce).' The story of Eve, she is happy to announce, was a fable, and woman was in no way responsible for the problems of the universe. 'Each month the ovum undertakes an extraordinary expedition from the ovary through the Fallopian tubes to the uterus, an unseen equivalent of going down the Mississippi on a raft or over Niagara Falls in a barrel. One might say that the activity of ova involved a daring and independence absent in fact, from the activity of spermatozoa, which move in jostling masses, swarming out on signal like a crowd of commuters from the 5.15. From this one can only conclude that women must be the more daring, individualistic and imaginative sex. '

Watch out! You may meet a <u>real</u> castrating female! But no need to worry at the moment girls don't drop handkerchiefs any more. They just ask for a light. And there's more than one way to pick up that one. You can fumble with matchbook. The kind with the correspondence school offer on it. Or you can thrust one of those two-buck stained steel lighters at her. Girls really flip for the delicate scent of lighter fluid. When you squeeze the trigger a long tapered flame pops up and a tiny thermostat keeps it adjusted at the perfect height. Automatically. And that happens a good 3,000 times before you refill. In your hand it has heft. But in your pocket it doesn't bulge.

It sounds like I'm totally uninvolved like being a ski-instructor in Berlin during World War II. His photographic image is of a man taking a shower with his suit and vest on. But he can peel off his raw hide jacket and reveal a shirt that seems to be cut from an American flag. And he displays all the external verities, the straining for vanished youth, the mindless drive, the conflict of narcissism and self-loathing. But since he begins at a manic, deafening leve, he has nowhere to grow. His manner combined the passion of an Iberian mystic with the humbled pride of a man

reduced to sweeping hospital corridors. And as for her - well she reforms herself, to customize herself, she has her face and body chopped and channelled. Her skin burnt off with chemicals to remove freckles, having her nose pruned, her face lifted and rearranged. A plastic surgeon blew up her breasts with silicone, and then because they did not please her deflated them again. A plastic surgeon on the make who talks more like a highway engineer than a mad scientist.

He tried on his faces in the rear-view mirror: a health faddist and sometime plumbing engineer and now an itinerant diemaker on his way out. He followed his X-wife and her lover past a sign: CENTRE FOR STUDIES OF THE BODY AND THE SOUL. Ah perhaps here at last... An offer to return to the delights of the primordial olfactory and tactile nitty-gritty.

The Virgin

It's his first flight. He's prepared for just about anything. But he's seldom ready for what he finds
> The silk jacket to lounge in
> The cool drink to lounge with
> The slippers we slide on his feet
> The sleep-mask when he wants to be alone
> We like to watch him giving in to the soft
> smile of our sari-clad girls
> And blushing a little over joined hands.
> First time should always be a little magic,
> don't you think.

Not long ago, he was considered an artful managerial mechanism, oiled with serenity, unanimity and self-confidence. Now he shows symptoms of severe internal distress. Like the plotybus, a semiaquatic egg-laying mammal this situation should not work but it does. Part love story part lecture in existential psychoanalysis and part rumination on the frayed boot-straps of mankind.

163

Groupe Grope and the feely show divided into two
environments. A passage jammed with bandaged,
bloodied black furry forms bound with rope. He who
successfully navigates this Scylla and Charybdis
will be treated to a carpet display including authentic
Middle Eastern rugs 'flayed human skin' and transparent
plastic mats stuffed with pig foetuses and viscera.
Coffins piled high with fresh innards offer contrast and
comparison to the salted intestines dangling from the
ceiling. Islamic music and the smell of rotting flesh
will fill the air. To discourage Exhibit nibblers wine
and barf bags are offered as refreshments. 2 nude and
squishy chicks lie on the floor to be walked on - like
carpets. Inspired by the evening he prowled and pranced
and minced randily for a lot of the time. As she danced
to some spoken poetry about something rising like a
tulip and falling like spaghetti. She stretched her arms
high and then let them dribble down.

He entered close behind them. It seemed they had been
to this place before. He noticed they were let through
without the bag of questions that were presented to
him:
'Your name?'
'Your trauma?'
'What do you hope to gain from these workshops?'

A guy with a toothpick-thin moustache. He had a
hangdog air about him and obviously favoured suits
with that pipe-rack look. His voice rarely rising above
a confidential whisper. 'This was not,' he emphasized
'a school but merely a sharing of experience and training
techniques, the better to help us understand one
another. We observe, discuss, and ask questions about
each others' traumas, in addition to demonstrating our
own.'

Last week you forgot three appointments. Yesterday
you almost lost an account. Today you went to sleep

dictating. And tomorrow... Tomorrow you just
may blow your stack.

I was worried that I somehow wouldn't get past this
inquisitor as he went on whispering 'Most of us are
self-prisoners cut off from our potential being. We
don't talk. We produce shit in three brands: rat shit,
cat shit and elephant shit. Our intellect is an ever-
chattering computer that splits us. We don't allow
ourselves to FEEL. In the workshops our aim is to
stop the cortical chatter and open the flow of
existence. Lose your mind, and come to your senses.
We seek to restore the mind's connection with natural
rhythms within and without, to loosen the intellect's
controlling grasp and free it for discovery. Don't push
the river it flows by itself. If you try to make the
semen flow, it turns into piss. ' I heard someone shout
out 'Keep your hands off me you world wide weirdo and
go get yourself fucked in the arse by the Greeks. I just
want to be noticed not attacked. ' I found one of my
voices shouting to my inquisitor 'I enjoy power, but
can play the good shepherd as well as the next man. I
lust - and am in fact in a semi-permanent state of
erection but fear retribution perhaps you can help
me?'

They separately enter a room and take facing seats.
But neither knows the other is there; an opaque screen
3 feet high stands between them obscuring the view.
All that each person has been told is that he/she will
meet someone and be expected to carry on an erotic
conversation with him. Abruptly, the screen is lifted,
and they confront each other across a bed. Will the
dominant or the submissive one avert his eyes first?
When his nerves begin humming like high tension wires,
when he takes his emotional temperature every other
minute and throws a night-long temper tantrum, the
dramatic results are explosively and corrosively alive.

When I looked at my inquisitor again he was saying 'You don't riot against your enemies, but against your friends, I know your type, because you know your friends don't shoot.' Just then a woman walked by in a nylon tricot panty with sheer side inserts and a contour padded fanny. The guy went on 'Where can you buy imagination? There's a special corner of the world filled with whimsy nothing you're likely to need, but we know you'll find something you won't want to live without in our little land of oddities.' His performance had a consciously archaic quality about it. He satirized fustian while indulging in it. His solemnity was a species of burlesque. I imagined he was a man of stupefying inconsistency always fond of quoting Emerson on the hobgoblin of little minds. And that he was shamelessly sentimental in his garden tending prize roses, poinsettias and camellias. On the other hand he could have been a physical fitness addict, pressing a 53-pound baseball in his office. 'Your capitulation is cheerfully satisfying - what's missing is the wildness within.' He whispered. In projecting the stillness of mental vacancy - the slow grin and steady gaze, the turn of a head that knows everything and nothing - he walks on eggshells and never breaks his stride. 'You know something you don't deserve to frolic here. You came in on the end and refused to suffer the years of mediocrity. You're spoiled. Not young enough, not old enough to suffer indignity, a pompous bastard on middle ground afraid of enduring awkward growing pains, preferring to settle for safe second place and lose a beautiful "now" for a distant "then".' He obviously enjoyed bringing a missionary zeal and a sense of genuine moral outrage to his oratory. What could I say?

Behind him I saw a room carpeted in gold and orange with 25 grey and hefty ladies lying in variegated pastel tights, slowly moving their limbs through the air. A

dozen people sat in a circle on the floor. Lying in the middle was my X-wife. 'Her karma has been messed up we have to locate the spirit. ' The whole group slid nearer and placed their hands on her body. Someone asked 'Where do you feel it?' 'In my stomach and thighs, ' she answered. 'Oh boy - I want you to just breathe in and out, really hard. ' Everybody pressed down on her body. 'You're hurting my stomach, ' she groaned. 'Ah see the spirit is out, ' and the group brushed 'it' away with ostrich plumes. 'All you have to do now is live, ' and she limped away. He smiled 'see it works every time. Our workshop is the new psychological frontier we teach Meanintperel or "Meaningful interpersonal relationships" and this is the Holy Grail of the psyche-orientated. Life is visceral rather than intellectual and the most visceral practitioners of life are those characterizing themselves as intellectuals. ' He went on and invoked parental prerogative. 'They need authority at some point and when they don't get it they're unhappy. ' I noticed he kept a buzzer panel under the lip of the table with one button marked 'coffee', another 'root beer', a third 'Fesca'. 'Come I'll show you around. '

I followed him through many rooms. He tape-recorded everything, aiming his microphone at conversations, monologues, freak-outs, and stream of consciousness raps. Certain moments stood out with clarity and boldness: a writhing tower of women barely discernible in the opening darkness. I thought at one stage I saw Nightripper mincing in puzzlement with upside-down helmets on his feet and a parasol. A hefty woman came on with huge balls under her dress for obscene dream-breasts-and-arse. They howled and pondered, loved and arranged and hated. A flood of encounters and impressions. In one room on a stage someone tap-danced and took off a lot of clothes while music played and the bombing of Pearl Harbor was radioed.

Roomfuls of girls and in their separate orbits were
sometimes difficult to attend to as a monologue in a
monotone, and the moments when they impinged on
each other became exclamation points. 'And in here
is a lecturer talking about "Erotica, Ennui and Where
Do We Go From Here". We entered and would you
believe that he didn't tell us? In fact I think he thought
that mentioning all the words in the title at least three
times each would keep him ahead of the game. 'And
in here we have instant analysis and querulous
criticism.' As soon as I entered someone shouted at
me 'You have an anarchical mentality totally rejecting
civilized standards of behavior.' And someone else,
why goddammit there she was my one and only first
X-wife supple and limber as a cat, a swift predatory
cat like a cheetah, and with the equivalent speed. She
had a cat's delicate equilibrium, which made off-
balance movements seductive. She contorted her
flexible torso and articulate hips into a restless
kaleidoscope. But my inquisitor led me on into yet
another room 'and here we have well as you can see
they could be lovers - but they are father and daughter
and by the time her commonlaw husband joins them it
will be clear that it all becomes Electra'. 'And how about
the father-son relationship?' 'Ah yes reduced to a
sequence of trips to movies, museums and zoos, the
bribe of sweets and presents for affection - the heart-
sickening estrangement gap - is that your trauma?'

As the wrangle intensifies he alleviates the strain with
scenes of a vanishing existence - of undisturbed salt
flats, of a newborn lamb on the grass, of vast,
unsaturated skies. It is here that his affectations are
replaced by affections. Should I tell him of the wife who
could Karate-chop hell out of me? But he took my arm and
led me yet into another room. 'And here we have
pathologically petulant nihilists likely to call down a
wave of right-wing repression upon themselves and

168

everyone else although we do not consider them to be a present threat against the order institutions of our workshops. ' He went up to a phosphorescent waif and asked her about sex 'I have nothing to say on that subject except to say, if one wishes to talk about bodily functions, fill what's empty, empty what's full and scratch where it itches. ' 'She is a housewife and a prisoner of her split-level home and Spock-directed family and trying so earnestly to rear her own little prodigy that she has lost her femininity in the process. Meanwhile the child ends up with guilt and the husband pursues his emasculating "career" to support the family, ' he said, holding the microphone under my chin, he obviously expected me to say something. 'Well when the action is hot, keep the rhetric cool I always say. ' As I glimpsed my X-wife again like a flickering peep show inflecting the movements with every bump and grind and twist and devouring space as if the room were a cage. Hardly a smile or a frown disrupted the still, dispassionate face. Her body though was on fire, moving as if possessed with an abandon that was reckless, the face as cool as the goddess Diana, the body as hot as Venus. 'Come I want to introduce you to a psychiatrist who is using astrology to guide his therapy sessions. ' I was introduced and he said 'Ah Libra with Scorpio rising you have a suppressed natural instinct to smash the enemy with a club or go after him with a meat axe. ' He was obviously one of those eager Mid-western emigrees who dote on Eastern intellectuals. I also had the feeling that he'd read one of those books called 'It Pays to Expand Your Word Power', and I think he kept using those words because he knew they got attention. He told me that I was a compulsive monologist who alternates between flip quips and narcissistic arias of self-pity. The interspersing of frequent asides and stream-of-consciousness speeches creating the undramatic effect of a man too busy commenting

169

on his life than living it. Revenge comes to him with
painful thought not bitter sweetness, but history comes
to him also with a bump-bump under the blazing sun,
and his day is done, and he exits laughing.

In the gardens I was immediately grabbed by the arm by
a freaked out guy who thought he was the Messiah, 'I
have written this book on world peace and it confirms
that I am the Messiah. I had a vision a year and a half
ago that I was being crucified, the purpose of the dream
was to reveal to me that I am the re-incarnation of
Jesus. Now all the old die-hard hippies who are addicted
to sado-masochism and immorality are persecuting me
after I converted to the Ten Commandments and non-
rebellious God rejecting behaviour. I am at war out here
with everyone - they want to subconsciously dwell in
hell-consciousness instead of heavenly nirvana
consciousness.' He didn't say whether his book would
appear in hardback, paperback or stone tablets. As I
walked on through the gardens I saw a few people lying
on a huge vinyl mattress filled with water, I joined
them and found it was like lolling on the stomach of a
mammoth dog, like floating on water without getting wet.
Soft, warm and occasionally it gurgled. My body was
completely supported which meant that no one got
squashed in the group activities, I just sank right in.
There was soft piped music, and had somehow a
reassuring hush. A woman attendant dressed in white
pantsuit and beige silk scarf, which later I discovered
was the uniform for the foundation's female staff,
directed us to close our eyes and sink right in. A few
of us did just that but others muttering, wriggled
around. One man next to me, about 75 years old and
laden with radical buttons said that he wanted to learn
more about himself so he could write his autobiography.
Another, about 50 years old, told how he and his wife
involved in women's lib, had worked out a wonderful
sex-life: she gets down on all fours, he enters her

from behind and she masturbates. Another guy overhearing this started on about his fear of masturbating which so far at the foundation they hadn't been able to reassure him 'it will grow hair on the palms of your hands and rot your brains out,' he whispered to me. Someone else shouted out suddenly 'Speak up or shut up. I have died in Viet Nam. But I have walked the face of the moon. Remember the good old days when only God would end the world? Now is the time for all good men to come to the aid of their planet. Do this or Die.'

I felt the beginning of a deep-set terror that they were all away on an ego trip of Shakespearian proportions that I could only watch moaning or huzzahing as they were inclined but thoroughly helpless to influence the course of the royal madness, an equivalent feeling of being there at the sunset of the long night. I felt if I said anything my voice would come from some odd and perilous psychic area still being charted, some basic metabolic flashpoint where the self struggles to convert its recurrent breakdowns into new holds on life and reality. His nervous system never betrayed him in the heat of battle. 'The test of leadership is whether one has the ability, as Kipling once said, 'to keep his head while others are losing theirs.' Not knowing how to act or not being able to act is what tears your insides out... But contrary to my usual instincts, I knew the correct course in this crisis was precisely to lean with the wind. The gentle slosh of air bubbles inside the mattress kept me quiet and almost contained and I started daydreaming even though the mutterings of those near me occasionally intruded.

At least Icarus put some wings on before he jumped off. He is a manic delight in the keyrole, twitching mutely when in despair, brassily egomanical in victory, and forever sniffing the air like a raunchy Shubert Alley cat. He is a monster with extraordinary size and strength and stamina. He is never given credit for exceptional performances or generous impulses. He is taken for granted as a brutal fact of nature, rebuked for his presumptions of humanity and sensitivity. At 43, he is a big bear of a man - 6ft. 3ins., 230 lbs. with the hard blue eyes of a riverboat gambler. He has strong fondness for the trappings of success: custom-built limousines with fur upholstery, 9 airplanes, 3,000 pairs of cuff links (many of them solid gold). His ranch encompasses 400 acres, a shooting gallery and a beauty parlour. What else could a man wish for? He wants to be a billionaire within 10 years. He manages his empire from an office protected against intruders by a uniformed guard, 6 secretaries and an electronically controlled door. The wood phone console beside his desk has 60 buttons, and a telephone hangs next to the urinal in his private toilet. Notices of in-coming calls boom through a two-way loudspeaker in the executive dining room. If a company official wishes to postpone answering, he merely lifts his head and bawls back his instructions to a microphone in the ceiling. In his rare leisure time, he takes safari trips in Africa. Personal popularity is important to the budding billionaire, who says, 'I want people to think well of me.'

I was cut short from my fantasizing by a woman bending over me. 'Male chauvinist pig. Have you told the blacks to have a sense of humour about their struggle for liberation?' Womens' lib again and not confined to revolutionary politics. He finds an unmade bed, a ring in the tub, and his little lady at a womens' lib rap group with the sisters. It smacks every cavalier straphanger who offers up his patch of plastic on the 'A' train, and instead of a coy eyebrow and licked lip, receives a stare that would ice up the Nile. She informed me she could have an absolutely gorgeous

clitoral orgasm in exactly 31 seconds, all by herself.
I told her to 'go ahead'.

Take the male chauvinist-pig test: Do you flinch more
when a woman gets socked in the mouth than when a
man does? Are you uneasy at how 'aggressive and
un-feminine' your woman editor is behaving? Or a
woman lawyer? Or a Weatherwoman? The electric
flashes between women's liberation and male chauvinism
are now the consuming revolutionary struggle. The
single bathroom is open to both sexes, and on its
anonymous walls are penned little dialectical nuggets
that would bring a blush to the cheeks of Masters &
Johnson and Brunnhilde's war-whoop to any half-
baked feminist. After a tussle with one member of
Womens' Lib, an eminent Boston psychiatrist said
'This lack of discipline is disgusting.' He spot-
diagnosed the woman as 'a paranoid fool and a stupid
bitch'. Another woman took the floor and began
relating her psychiatric history. 'The doctor likened me
to a borderline schizophrenic,' she cried in indignation.
A psychiatrist in the audience called, 'You're past the
borderline now.'

I rolled over and found myself practically on top of an
enormous woman who giggled and whispered in my ear
'whenever someone touches me I'm in love with him
for about eight hours.' 'Excuse me M'am' I replied and
attempted to move away. 'I chose you because I thought
it out in my stomach. In here all you have are instincts'
she replied as she nudged nearer. I was filled with how-
do-I-get-outta-here feeling, as she went on whispering
'help me to discover how I want to live - I'm going to
get rid of myself in stages - how about you?' I knew I
must look like Lady Chatterley's father without his
sense of humour. Like all nightmare images it inhabits
that place in you that it seems to have created purposely
for its own habitation, that place that did not exist
before it began always to be there. It was like I was the

observer in a drama going on without my life, thus
ultimately a drama not going on. I felt sure this chick
was a raging sado-masochist who sticks her breasts
into a light socket to experience the joys of electric-
shock torture. Why weren't there some groovey
pubescent Isadoras? If I stay on here I might end up
with some fire-breathing spinster screaming 'Masher'
at me bending her umbrella over me. Suddenly she
bounced up and stood surveying us all. Her rap was
a husky no-nonsense crisp and smart so this is what
you came to see so here I am type of commentary on
the package she's delivering. 'The devil has sent me
here to make tricks among all you lunatics Miss Kicks
yeah that's what I am and don't you forget it hey why
donchu shit up so you can see me better. I want
everyone to see me the way I am.' I was transfixed by
her chin where all the fear and tension was concentrated
in a kind of moronic half open lockjaw look. Then lower
down I saw she was a silicone freak with breasts large
enough to halt both traffic on Wall Street and arousal
on 42nd Street. Some of the group got up from the
mattress and began dancing. It was as if they were
trying to get the feel of some kind of nameless horror.
At first hurling themselves in crazy tumbling flights,
committing violence upon each other - seemingly out
of terror, not even seeing what they were doing. One
guy moved in a shambling style - as if to suggest the
lack of control or unfocus of sleep, while others
around him became armchairs or tables when needed.

I moved out and went into the workshop building where
I was shown my room, but no sooner was I installed
than two cats invaded, I yelled, 'Fuck and shit crap
and corruption carnation get this animal carnival out
my goddam room.' He used a heightened pantomime
often casts himself as the little man beset by terrors
and nightmares in the privacy of his room. One thing
they have to know are the subtle signals that man

'stay away cool it your riding on too hard!'. But they remained and I realized they were therapists after one of them declared, 'his main problem is guilt over a galloping voyeurism along with secondary problem of a rejecting mother, not so much a desire for innocence as an attempt to re-capture the lost milk/love-giving breast of childhood.' Sideburned therapist No. 2 saw my problem as 'an inability to love. Afraid to get close to people especially women, he must treat them as objects of his imagination - a role that implies both control and distancing. His narcissism is his attempt to regain the lost omnipotence of childhood.' Therapist No. 1, balding and older than the other, considered me something of a 'compulsive liar'. His particular insight: 'We've all heard a lot about penis envy, but what about its opposite?' Therapist No. 2 came up with 'manic-depressive hysteric'. No. 1 went on as if he had exhausted his analysis of me, 'We had headaches for a while, but we took care of them. The armpit had its moment of glory, and the toes, with their athlete's foot. We went through wrinkles, we went through diets. We conquered haemorrhoids. So what's left - the vagina. Today the vagina, tomorrow the world.' He went on like a blue streak. He spoke not to me but at me, in fact to a point somewhere direct behind my shoulder or just above my head. The talk quick, sharp, clever, a dazzling display of brilliance which indeed was remarkable, and enormously pleasurable; but it left me numb, as though I had been spayed. I was unable to respond; a desperate competitiveness around me what could I say that would justify an interruption to all that verbal glory? Finally it was all simply too diffuse. I could understand if I were made to feel it, the terrible figure of Kali, I could understand a kind of Lawrencian blood sacrifice, I could understand if I were made to feel it, the marvellous serenity of Krishna love. I needed to feel the premises inundated with the Terrible Mother and the serene

compassionate Krishna I needed to be shaken by
terror and love. An attempt explicit, ardent, heroic
perhaps, though at best only half successful - to
perform the most necessary task: to connect the past
with the future. Suddenly the door opened and my No.
2 X-wife entered. Was I dreaming, was this really
someone who looked like her?

No. It was her alright, walking in twisting little
circles, like a caged animal. Not really a wild animal,
but a poorly domesticated one petulant rather than
fierce, caught in a thicket of heavy-legged furniture.
At one moment of electric outrage upon seeing me she
raised clenched fists to heaven like Antigone, then
slowly lowered them to her neck, like just another
housewife with just another nagging backache. A
compassionately balanced mood-portrait of modern
woman: boredom at the level of panic, a yawn that
comes out a scream. I felt like some Chinese water-
torturer coming back again and then again to the death
tolls, the waste, the ashen priorities that favour death
to life. Fear rides on his back like a schizoid chimp.
His voice climbs from neurotic to hysterical - and
winds back down again, without missing a moan. On his
tortured face is a look of applied sanity that befits only
saints and madmen. He walks through a closed system
to which everyone but the dreamer has a key. Like a
spiral staircase set with mirrors. He ascends by units
of pain, glimpsing pieces of himself until he comes to
a landing of incomprehension. He moves numbly through
it all, reminiscent of the Steinberg drawing in which
a rabbit peers out of a human face.

One of the most trying experiences an individual can
go through is the period of doubt, of soul-searching, to
determine whether to fight the battle or to fly from it.
It is in such a period that almost unbearable tensions
build up, tensions that can be relieved only by taking
action, one way or the other. And significantly, it is

176

this period of crisis conduct that separates the leaders from the followers. A leader is one who has the emotional mental and physical strength to withstand the pressures and tension created by necessary doubts and then, at the critical moment, to make a choice and act decisively. The men who fail are those who are so overcome by doubt that they either crack under the strain or flee to avoid meeting the problem at all. On the other hand if one is to act and to lead responsibly he must necessarily go through this period of soul-searching and testing of alternate courses of action, otherwise he shoots from the hip, misses the target and loses the battle through sheer recklessness. One must always be keyed up for battle but he must not be jittery; he is jittery only when he worries about the natural symptoms of stress. Those who have known great crisis - its challenge and tension, its victory and defeat - can never become adjusted to a more leisurely and orderly pace.

'Well you finally made it what do you think of the place full of madcaps, egomaniacs and fuckups - who can ask for more?' My second X-wife said and went on, 'Yeah last week I bought a rifle for self-protection. Up here you gotta be nice or they'll get you. ' I became the classic rip-off-hip example with a heavy 'peace, love, far out wow-man-like-it's-so-beautiful' rap. He isn't Super Hippie. He is glossily authentic and is issuing his freak facade with a specific goal in mind. 'Of course there is a high-risk activity, though I haven't yet fallen off the bridge, ' I managed to say to her. I couldn't help thinking that memory is more or 'less arranged', but the placed elements level one another, displace instead of pressuring towards specific focus, attenuate so that one senses things slipping from one. Every so often one senses an unhinging in the continued banality of a movement, and also at intervals there's the possibility of one's nightmare creations summoning one to them.

The tendency to fulfil an impulse is not especially illuminating. Thrusting normally uncomplementary forces together, battling the initial impulse, allows the possibility of entering new psychological terrain. The situation badly needs dislodging elements. I noticed she was still able to isolate areas of her body beautifully, and that pair of conjuror's eyes! Enough to throw me into a Dionysian fantasy. But instead I caught myself wondering: why, yesterday (last month, last year) things were better. Or even: yesterday last year, I was an entirely different person. I am dulled before the fact of death; not by its absence, but by its omnipresence. And there he came - a little chubby a toneless voice, but those steady eyes, that sense of hidden power. Was there something here after all? Those teeth and that Viking countenance weren't enough. He came across wooden, a fugitive from a high school rhetoric class, arms shooting out stiffly, phrases as self-conscious as the morning after. Tried to keep it moderate, walk that middle line. Only that's where the enemy was. He wished he had learned how to offer a cheek and withdraw a psyche.

Meanwhile the therapists said not a word, but watched closely, I guess, our reactions. Information is being collected into data banks by the Army, the Justice Department and the F.B.I. The Judge declared that the Army is not 'doing anything newspapers are not doing - keeping information in their morgues'. I had the feeling that the whole place was an inbred life, a life turned in on itself, I had the uneasy feeling also that people talked to themselves, in a language devised for each other, delivered in papers written for each other, at conferences held for each other, supported by agencies formed for each other. And all done in the self-important atmosphere of addressing themselves to the problems of the world, which is their responsibility to find solutions for. Where finally all the men have

crocodile wives and ulcers and gold-and-diamond rings
that twist around their hairy fingers.

I kissed my No. 2 X-wife and said goodbye. I wanted
out. To be on the chase again. Remember the fun you
used to have? Life for the lucky folks still has the
old razz-a-matazz. There's dancing and golf and
bridge and swimming and lawn bowling and crafts and
shuffle-board and other things like sitting in the sun
and discussing the future. I took a last look at my No.
2 X-wife she stood three feet away, watching me. I
waved. She smiled. A sun I could not feel brightened
her hair. A sea breeze I could not savour ruffled it.
I wish I could have joined her, for I have returned from
a strange journey into an alien world. Unhappily I
couldn't. That undersea realm I have visited is exacting
its price of admission. Living in the depth. I have
become in certain ways a creature of those depths,
adapted to their pressures. Now the human environment
is temporarily intolerable to me. And so I must wait
inside this life-saving prison until I have been weaned
from pressure and made once more fit to live on earth.

I left a note for my No. 1 X-wife before leaving: I
request an interview at such time and place as you may
designate, to discuss the terms of surrender. I could
just hear her lover's reply, 'Well, so you have
surrendered. Couldn't you have taken to the hills and
carried on for a year or more?' I thought of extending
the note telling her that I always thought she'd look
beautiful in a cheongsam. But instead decided to take
two parts of insight and three parts of gall. Combined
with chunks of meaty research, seasoned with flammable
forecasts and served sizzling on a sharpened verbal
skewer.

Back on the road again. Where had they got to? A
deserted freeway. No. Wait. A solitary figure in the
distance. An Indian. Though if it hadn't been for his

turqoise head-band, heavy necklaces, the darker colour of his skin, hair, eyes, he would hardly have looked an Indian. His face bore the hard lines of the harsh weather. His hair was short, combed back, and he wore the simple clothes of a rancher. He waved me down. Well why not, perhaps he'd take me somewhere. Somewhere no one would ever find me. I'd live a simple life with an Indian tribe, learn the medicine man's trade. Live out my visions, dreams. I asked him where he was heading. He pointed west. He was soft-spoken, no preliminaries, but talked as if to himself. 'I was praying for my people, and I had a dream I was in a kiva. I saw a fire, blue and green, in the dark at the far side. I knew it was a presence. I knew it was the supreme being. He was covered with eagle feathers. He had a beak like an eagle and a body like a man. He said to look to the left. I looked and saw stone tablets with pictographs. He said, look there and you'll find the answer. They said, in the last days my tribe would be the last to go. That's happening now, so we know the time is close. For hundreds of years, the large star followed the small star across the sky. And the Great Spirit said when the stars reverse the time is right. That happened two months ago. He also said that we should go out and meet people to see who is true and who is not true. And that's what I am doing.'

I felt his dark eyes on me. Was I being summed up, would he find I was one of the true ones? Classic shaped, carved out of a solid block of gold? Inside solid, pressure-proof walls of my oyster soul a self-winding officially certified chronometer movement, no longer willing to suffer a steady loss of energy through over-work and age. A thinking man, using the results of up-to-date research to rebuild my reserves of natural energy. Hidden reserves of strength. A well balanced formula revives the whole organism from within, attacking every adventure from fox hunting to mountain climbing with uncompromising verve, recycling all kinds of waste. A cosy system capable of enormous dynamism. Though his ideas seem to belong more to the realm of fantasy than fact he manages nonetheless to stimulate the imagination and guide the mind to areas of persuasive charm that is both abstract and real, and reflects Faust's gallant laughter in the face of evil. He'll remember details like lace sleeves he's seen in a Flemish masterwork, expand them into blown-up patterns, offset with gingham checks from his wife's summer dress, and counterpoint both with huge pointillist dots until he had conjured up a rabbit-hole view of a Wonderland garden. No delays, no strange consultations, and no funny looks. Even in the most remote places, such memories are familiar and absolutely trusted. The result is a rare observation of the pathos and humour engendered by the rites of man. No hit-and-run villain, but wistful, tentative, he may be unsure of the proper words to say, but he knows enough to do the right thing, he can convey more with a lowered eyelid than most men do with a shrug of their shoulders. Though at times he sees himself as a punk and a sucker who has never got anything from a society filled with takers, he feels a compulsion to prove his manhood. Sometimes even brainpower has its limits. He looked into a mirror and asked himself: Was I brainwashed? Would I think I was brainwashed if I had been brainwashed? But behind all these gigantic dimensions lies an immeasurable mystery, perhaps for reasons beyond your control, you may find your identity is not building up as fast as you expect it to. He so ignores the canons of construction that at times he seems involved in little more than an engagement in a shaggy-dog story. Plainly believing that he lives in God's country. He may even be trying to provide some benevolent fat deity with a blueprint for his own future return, as the apotheosis of the anti-hero, fondling a missile as if it were a kitten.

Inside the complacent optimist a desperate pessimist
is signalling wildly to get out to hammer at the door
of the better living club and getting no reply. As the
problems grow in number and complexity, so do the
answers: From a simple Yes or No to a not-so-simple
multiplicity of choice. You'll see a hundred wonders.
Wild game, and thatch-roof tukuls. The result evokes
the tragedy of a sleepwalker who can be awakened only
by Rokushingan, ingredients of which are musk, liquid
from toad, roots of Korean carrot, aloe wood extracts,
powder of cultured pearl congealed cow gall and
genuine bile of bears. Rare as in
gold
pale as in gold
pure, as in gold
finer
Finer in taste
Smooth, not rough. Pale, not dark.
With yet a silky strength
that belies its gentle nature.
His arms thrust exuberantly into the air like a
victorious matador who had just been awarded two ears
and a tail. The methods he proposes for dealing with
the Enemy are fiendishly sophisticated. No simple
stapling, folding or mutilation, but carefully cutting
out three or four extra rectangular holes with a razor
blade. Most of his life he pushed himself at such a
headlong pace into anything new - a new project, a
new theory, a new friendship - that he often seemed to
be on the verge of a nervous breakdown. His role is
to sting minds, being provocative rather than profound.
A life of dazzling transitions that sometimes makes
him seem unstable. A life so intense must exact its
costs. Tidy and appealing as such hypotheses may
seem, enormous obstacles stand in the way of their
becoming reality.

Never had I felt more of a punk. As if this Indian could

detect the numberless ludicrous incidents, the
infinitely dull stupid indulgent anglo I really was. But
perhaps he wasn't an Indian at all. Some hippy having
me on. All part of the conspiracy. They had bribed
him to lead me to instant death. Suddenly I felt as
though trapped in the last car of the Subway. Beaten,
unable to escape, my screams unheard as the car
goes through dark subterranean tunnels. What could
be more calculated to put me more up-tight? Scary
stuff. Like violence in a hallway - or an elevator.
Bound to have a knife tucked away, perhaps in boots,
or head gear. The sequence concludes with a lingering
shot of the man's naked body hurtling to its doom,
buttocks gleaming.

I took quick glances at him. He stared fixedly ahead,
or into some dream-landscape of his own. At the same
time I noticed in the mirror that they had crept up on
me. 'They are false those who follow you, ' the Indian
quietly said. My hands gripped the wheel in an attempt
to stop them shaking. What could I do - say? I remained
grimly silent, and stepped up the gas. My companion
closed his eyes. I longed to do likewise. Be done with
it all, and roll smoothly towards the West. Perhaps
he was waiting for just this opportunity. Revenge. Not
only my head. But theirs also. The landscape closed
in. Petrified trees exposed by erosion scattered on
the desert floor. 'Here the blue-throated hummingbird
is worshipped. ' His soft voice startled me. I nodded,
as if I knew all about the worship of blue-throated
hummingbirds. What I really pictured were the faint
blue veins between my X-wife's thighs, standing out,
as a group of half naked Indians strung her up over a
fire, their knives flashing, eyes glinting. And the
blood gushing from her warbling throat. Again a
balance is struck, but a much lower level of destructive
capability. But she's safe, with power assisted front
disc brakes, laminated safety windshield, dual braking

system and four-way warning flashers. Hadn't she predicted the melting of the polar ice caps followed by catastrophic floods, and discussed the presence of DDT in the flesh of Antarctic penguins?

She moves so easily with such knowing grace, she walks in metric beauty, through her mellowing lover's elegant world, through it and beyond at last to younger, stronger, more passionate arms. But then she goes back to her husband. Did half of me want her back? No. No. Remember marriage, any relationship with a woman is a gruelling, dehumanizing trial. It is repeating the same familiar phrases again and again, accepting vicious abuse with a grin, and living in a fishbowl without privacy or time for introspection. The moments of high drama and decisive confrontation are rare. The face-to-face debates, the adrenalin-liberating rallies in bed, and the euphoria that follows are just the glamorous top of the iceberg. Mostly marriage is dull meetings, petty intrigues, tranquillising repetition and exhausting hours of uncertain results, and eating hotdogs all day. Nothing but belching and burping. Watch him stagger to his door. His wife will kill him. Should have been home hours ago. Dinner cold. She'll kill him. But what about the lives of the figures who sit behind the wheel in ads for new cars? She is dressed all in yellow. She's smiling at the hot day, the gleaming chromium. She is blonde and tall and tanned. Tennis and surfing and yachting. She's gorgeous. The guy is dressed in hardware glinted crinkle jacket to the highrise deep pleated tweed trousers held up by suspenders so bright you can almost hear them coming. And that white-on-white body-shirt. He's grinning to the heat. Blonde and tall and tanned. Tennis and surfing and yachting. He's gorgeous. Everyone will be perfect. Even if you take them by moonlight.

Suddenly I wanted to talk, tell my companion everything. As if my days were numbered. But he was asleep, gently snoring. And I noticed they were no longer following. I slowed down. 'If you take the next exit you'll come to where we can stop off for a while,' the Indian said, his eyes still closed. I turned off, and he directed me onto a dusty track, winding over barren land. Soon he would take out his knife and... Two more Indians waved me down. Now three of them sat in the back, blankets over their heads and shoulders. The smell of bourbon filled the car. Through rising clouds of sand I saw a huddle of adobes on top of a high mesa. I was motioned to stop the car. As though hypnotised I obeyed, and followed the three between rocks and cactus towards the village.

As if my presence had been forewarned, I heard a drum vibrating, like some huge heart beating away underground, which indeed made the earth shake slightly. Women and children squatted on the flat adobe roofs. No one took any notice of us as we walked on into a crowded plaza where two columns of half naked, painted Indians danced. Their feet pounded into the sand arena. Women's hair swayed in the whirling dust, their eyes lowered. Three or four strange looking Fellini figures, hair and body covered with clay, stood on the kiva. I realised if I'd wanted to leave it would have been impossible. I was surrounded. So this is it. Well what better way to croak. Ritualistic, part of an inheritance, I would perhaps go down in history after all. Much better, perhaps more original say than being crushed to death in some squalid freakout, a monstrous Dionysian revel, where a mob of crazies gather to drop acid and groove to hours of amplified cacophany. So here I was, suddenly it seemed without past or future on a flat sandy floor, 7,500 feet above sea level, encircled by steep mountain walls, not unlike one of the great dry seas of the moon. And as I walked it seemed I had no sense of gravity. My pulse, I noticed, kept up the same rhythm as the drums. I was led through

185

the vast crowd, until we were so near the dancers I
saw the sweat on their faces and chests. Meanwhile
my three companions disappeared.

Clouds gathered and moved heavily over the mountains.
The wind rose, sand whirled up everywhere, but the
dancers held up their heads, and those at the end of the
two columns seemed to be part of the clouds, as if they
were ascending into the sky. My eyes bombarded by
elements. My body swayed to the drum rhythm. I felt
as though in a trance. Then I saw my X-wife, the other
side of the dancers. She leaned against one of the adobe
houses. And what a costume she had on! A black velvet
jumpsuit and matching maxi coat, shoes in black velvet
with satin straps, and trailing from her neck a mile
long white fringe scarf, more than long enough to lynch
me with. No doubt he was dressed in the coming colour
of purple. The resurgent pur or Argyle plaid, leggy
pants and a Banlon turtleneck starting from his chin
and going clear down to his dirty toenails. Or maybe he
was in a hooded catsuit? I jerked round expecting him
behind me. A thought occurred that their obvious
intention was not to hustle me to my destination until
I had understood the inevitability of my fate through a
series of rituals. It was all too much, as if here in a
strange environment I really couldn't cope. A mild
flip needed, in which my inner self could assert its
psychic energy and enable me to transcend it all.
Instead I remembered vividly a high school football
game when I got mauled by a 250-pound linebacker.
But this is certainly no time to create the impression
that we are turning back, but a time for pressing forward
with vigour. This is a time to say that time is running
out on me. I mentally concentrated on various parts of
my body, through sand-blown eyes. And remembered a
vivid dream I had of flying, waking from that fully
convinced I could fly, not that I made the attempt,
but the feeling floated through me, around all day,

giving me an almost contact high.

I edged back, and managed to squat behind a group of
women, but was instantly informed by their eyes I was
an intruder, an invader, a Real Estate speculator
jumping from bar to club to restaurant to hotel. Nice,
clean, modern sterile hotel. They were ancient witches,
where were the young ones to shout Hey there he is in a
super, supple antiqued leather jacket. It's got the
sexiest European snaps and straps. Ummmm, isn't he
great? Like Wow! I tried pushing my way back through
the crowd. This proved impossible. I looked round for
my Indian friend, where had he gone? I felt he was a
kind of guardian, that if he were with me I had nothing
to lose, nothing would be a threat. I looked at each of
the dancers, thinking perhaps he had joined them. But
realised I would hardly recognise him with paint over
his face. And where had my black velveted lyncher
gone? Had she seen me yet? I was twitching, hot.
My body weighed down, it seemed, from the sand. A
group of elders appeared and stood off-centre, in a
circle, beating the drum, and chanting. Rain started.
People moved into doorways. Others remained,
wrapping their blankets further over their heads. Bells
around the performers' ankles, between feathers, made
a music of their own. Fur pelts swayed from the men's
waists. From the side of the adobe buildings a strange
figure appeared. I was convinced that somehow not many
people, if any, but myself saw him. Dressed in black,
wearing a white mask, he carried a huge whip. He
stood off to the side for a moment, then disappeared. I
felt sure this had been my Indian friend, and decided
to follow him. Again it was difficult to make my way,
but soon I arrived in an alleyway. But shit there they
were, the lynchers, and holding their conspiracy in -
dammit - my car! I sprang back and leaned against a
ladder, which soon I began to climb. They would never
think of looking for me up there. You idiot you'll

187

obviously wear your grin to the grave. For once on the roof I realised I was in a more prominent position than ever, and sure enough they looked up and immediately he jumped out of the car. He had the rheumy eyes of a bloodhound, the jowls of a St. Bernard, and a baldachin of hair like that of an extraordinarily unkempt poodle. His face looked as if it had been slept in. I could even hear his voice, carried by the wind, a sesquipedalian vocabular, diapasonal sound like a Hammond organ in a dense fog.

Once the gesture is started it is impossible to hold it back. I knew I was initiating a long chain of circumstances but I had no idea where they might lead. I grabbed a blanket, and wrapped it over my shoulders and head. Climbing down the ladder I slipped and fell headlong. Half stunned I ran towards the plaza, and slowed down. Surely they would not recognise me now. My boots - a giveaway. A boot for the man who applies the same aplomb to his wardrobe that he does to his women. Glove-soft, leg-hugging baby calfskin, lined in kidskin. A concealed inside zipper makes it so clinging, you can wear it beneath narrowest pants. Note the oblique wafer-thin very-in square toe. Limited production. Should I take them off? No, in the crowd they would hardly be able to see that far. Moving cautiously I reached the other side of the plaza. Once there I breathed more freely. The whole thing had really reached a goddamned farce. Where for Christsake the movie cameras, and Bob Hope dressed as an Indian would surely appear in the midst of the dancers. What am I into? Party Games? Shit. Then I remembered my mother-in-law was a member of one of the new women's liberation groups: WITCH (Women's International Terrorist Conspiracy from Hell) - more guerrilla theatre than IRA; perhaps she had persuaded her daughter to become a member. Certainly her latest Swedish job of black velvet suited the role, though no doubt under it all she would inevitably smell of onions and Ajax.

I peered over heads, and noticed three strange figures had joined the dancers. They looked like the Spanish Inquisition, black witch hats, black masks, cloaks. They rode hobby horses, and they bobbed up and down on the outside of the dancers. Behind them walked the white masked figure I had seen earlier, waving his whip, and behind him on a red velvet awning a small idol of a saint swayed. A procession formed and moved out of the plaza towards the church. Soon the place was practically deserted, apart from some hungry looking dogs, and myself. The distant sounds of the drums. I was soon surrounded by the dogs. Growling, brown mangy looking monsters sniffing at my boots.

Maybe I should leave. Undecided I moved round the various houses, followed by the dogs. On my journey I took note that my car was no longer parked in the same place, but in another area, facing a main track. Rain was heavy. A few shadowy blanketed shapes passed, padding up and down ladders. A large group of men sat in a circle on the kiva roof, where a ladder leading into the kiva itself made two spires against the darkening sky. How unlike those iron stairs of the subway: the turnstile a symbol of authority, a meter of the capitalist system, a regulator of human movement, a metal-petalled flower of law and order. And like hell I was part of that system that turned men into well-fed and well-cared for pigs only interested in consumption and excretion. But secretly bearing the image of death-devoted Tristan - a modern day existential hero who is haunted by a world he can neither take nor leave. And this world? Here on an Indian Reservation, I felt more of an outsider. And the dogs knew. The buildings, part of the earth, made from earth, threw me into narrow spaces. Swept along by dust rain and wind. And longing for the comfort of four walls

a bed
sofa
marble-top table
thick beige rug
a bar made of walnut
ice cube needs from a humming machine
hot, cold and moving air
a choice of piped-in music, violin or saxophone
a yellow-panelled armoire to open and present TV in
colour
a marble lavatory
electric outlets for a shave and brushing the teeth with
eclat
a square porcelain block inside frosted glass with a
diagonal depression for bathing, a vertical rail to
prevent tilting, a horizontal bar down low to get up by
and a phone by the toilet seat for receiving calls at
odd moments.

I climbed up to one of the roofs. An open door. A long
table laiden with food, wooden bowls of delicious
smelling food, around which men sat, laughing, talking,
while women came and went, bearing more food, taking
away empty bowls, plates. I recognised my Indian
friend. I went nearer. Heard a coyotee howl, and another
answer in the distance. I pulled the blanket further
over my head and retreated. Let him find truer friends,
the stars for myself will never reverse.

I was about to climb down when I noticed two black
shrouded figures climbing up. They were the Inquisition,
still wearing their masks. One looked up, paused, and
said something to the other conspirator. I staggered
back. Those eyes! Hardly those of an Indian. But the
feline eyes of one dedicated to WITCH. Ah what next?
No time to think. Defeat is an orphan, victory has a
thousand fathers. I ran from roof to roof, the dogs
barked and began leaping after me. Below, lanterns
were swinging, as people emerged. Followed by shouts.

Soon not only the dogs pursued me. I came to the edge
of a roof. A space. Darkness. A revolutionary jump.
There should have been a photograph of it. History
caught with stoop-action camera. And in that darkness
I stretched out a physical life of taut muscalature. Slow,
deliberate movements, at times almost slow motion,
analogous to the mental pressure on me in the grip of
frightful uncertainty. Perhaps I had been mistaken, they
had not disguised themselves at all, but had split, left
me to find my own death. By chance. By an absurd piece
of my own fantasy. Hold it Mac. Silence. Shapes moved
from walls, proving to be only my own shadow. The dogs
had quietened down, disappeared in fact. I moved slowly
against the walls. Ghost-wormed my way past closed
doors, towards the place where I had last seen my car.
Of course it was no longer there. Shivering I made my
way towards the church, the only place I felt where I
could seek shelter without necessarily intruding. But
even there I felt uneasy, confronted by a small statue
of an Indian looking Christ. I sat on one of the wooden
benches, and closed my eyes.

Thoughtful and cautious, as if I needed to pay attention
to each element of the situation in an attempt at moment-
for-moment truth. Separating elements so as to put
them in isolation and relief. Eccentricities in their
most literal sense of approaching reality from an angle
somewhat off-centre. There must be detailed patient
exploration of evidence in support of an original
philosophical vision. Or on a humbler level simply
testing out propositions with data. Dissolving false and
ideological constructs about the world and letting reality
emerge as it really is.

Sitting there brooding, I discovered a breathing space,
but a space before the scream inside me was working
itself loose. A scream that came from a long series
of emotional changes. Fear for safety and sanity,
helplessness, frustration, and a desperate need to

break out into a stream of verbal images. The pulpit could become an extension of my voice, my skin, my dreams. Leaning over the wood, staring at the spluttering candles, the slanting eyes of the statues all around me, their shadows like kachina gods dancing in the walls of earth. Earth moving out into the world. I opened my mouth, but no words. Only the words of others I saw, like ads, texts, psalms, from those who had attempted to persuade me into their systems. A power I did not want to possess. The Inquisition.

Dear readers,

As well as relying on bookshop sales, And Other Stories relies on subscriptions from people like you for many of our books, whose stories other publishers often consider too risky to take on.

Our subscribers don't just make the books physically happen. They also help us approach booksellers, because we can demonstrate that our books already have readers and fans. And they give us the security to publish in line with our values, which are collaborative, imaginative and 'shamelessly literary'.

All of our subscribers:
- receive a first-edition copy of each of the books they subscribe to
- are thanked by name at the end of our subscriber-supported books
- receive little extras from us by way of thank you, for example: post-cards created by our authors

BECOME A SUBSCRIBER, OR GIVE A SUBSCRIPTION TO A FRIEND

Visit andotherstories.org/subscriptions to help make our books happen. You can subscribe to books we're in the process of making. To purchase books we have already published, we urge you to support your local or favourite bookshop and order directly from them – the often unsung heroes of publishing.

OTHER WAYS TO GET INVOLVED

If you'd like to know about upcoming events and reading groups (our foreign-language reading groups help us choose books to publish, for example) you can:
- join our mailing list at: andotherstories.org
- follow us on Twitter: @andothertweets
- join us on Facebook: facebook.com/AndOtherStoriesBooks
- admire our books on Instagram: @andotherpics
- follow our blog: andotherstories.org/ampersand

CURRENT & UPCOMING BOOKS

ANN QUIN (b. 1936) was a British writer from Brighton. She was prominent amongst a group of British experimental writers of the 1960s, which included B.S. Johnson. Prior to her death in 1973, she published four novels: *Berg* (1964), *Three* (1966), *Passages* (1969), and *Tripticks* (1972). A collection of her short stories and fragments, *The Unmapped Country* (edited by Jennifer Hodgson) was published by And Other Stories in 2018.